WICKED VILLAINS SHORTS

KATEE ROBERT

TRINKETS AND TALES LLC

ALSO BY KATEE ROBERT

Wicked Villains

Book 1: Desperate Measures

Book 2: Learn My Lesson

Book 3: A Worthy Opponent

Book 4: The Beast

Book 5: The Sea Witch

Book 6: Queen Takes Rose

A Touch of Taboo

Book 1: Your Dad Will Do

Book 2: Gifting Me To His Best Friend

The Island of Ys

Book 1: His Forbidden Desire

Book 2: Her Rival's Touch

Book 3: His Tormented Heart

Book 4: Her Vengeful Embrace

The Thalanian Dynasty Series (MMF)

Book 1: Theirs for the Night

Book 2: Forever Theirs

Book 3: Theirs Ever After

Book 4: Their Second Chance

The Kings Series

Book 1: The Last King

Book 2: The Fearless King

The Hidden Sins Series

Book 1: The Devil's Daughter

Book 2: The Hunting Grounds

Book 3: The Surviving Girls

The Make Me Series

Book 1: Make Me Want

Book 2: Make Me Crave

Book 3: Make Me Yours

Book 4: Make Me Need

The O'Malley Series

Book 1: The Marriage Contract

Book 2: The Wedding Pact

Book 3: An Indecent Proposal

Book 4: Forbidden Promises

Book 5: Undercover Attraction

Book 6: The Bastard's Bargain

The Hot in Hollywood Series

Book 1: Ties that Bind

Book 2: Animal Attraction

The Foolproof Love Series

Book 1: A Foolproof Love

Book 2: Fool Me Once

Book 3: A Fool for You

Out of Uniform Series
Book 1: In Bed with Mr. Wrong
Book 1.5: His to Keep
Book 2: Falling for His Best Friend
Book 3: His Lover to Protect
Book 3.5: His to Take

Serve Series
Book 1: Mistaken by Fate
Book 2: Betting on Fate
Book 3: Protecting Fate

Come Undone Series
Book 1: Wrong Bed, Right Guy
Book 2: Chasing Mrs. Right
Book 3: Two Wrongs, One Right
Book 3.5: Seducing Mr. Right

Other Books
Seducing the Bridesmaid
Meeting His Match
Prom Queen
The Siren's Curse

1

MEG'S APOLOGY

JASMINE

"**J**asmine."

I look up from the paperwork I've spent the last hour wading through. At this point, any interruption is a welcome one, if only to give me a break. Unsurprising to all, my father didn't keep the best of records. If it wasn't for Jafar's ambition—and organization skills—the whole feat would have been an impossible one.

As it is, I'm tired and irritable and all too happy to see Jafar walk through the door of the room I've converted to a study. I run my fingers through my hair and rise to meet him. "You look happy."

"I have a surprise for you."

My heart stutters and I examine his face. "A surprise." The last time he surprised me, I ended up with three cocks inside me at the same time. The memory of that heats my skin and it must linger in my eyes as well from the way Jafar's gaze narrows on me.

He slides his hands into his pockets, a sure sign that I'm about to end up on my knees. "If you'd like a repeat of that night, all you have to do is ask."

It's on the tip of my tongue to do exactly that. As much as I love my new role running my father's business during the day, I love my nights with Jafar just as much.

But it's not night at the moment, and unfortunately, I have far too much work to do before I can leave the study. "Soon."

Jafar watches me for a few moments, and it takes everything I have to hold still, to let him look despite every instinct screaming for me to run. I know how that ends. I *love* how that ends. I force an annoyed sigh that I don't feel. "You said you had a surprise. I still have to finish wading through the order shipments from last quarter."

"You could have someone else do it."

I give him the look that deserves. When it comes right down to it, he doesn't delegate any better than I do. There are numbers off with the shipments, and while some of the responsibility for that sits at Jafar's feet, I don't think all of it does. I refuse to be as lax as my father was—or as heartless. "Jafar, can this wait until tonight?"

"No." He reaches for the door. "Unfortunately, we're on a time limit and she has somewhere to be tonight."

She.

The door opens and there she is. Meg. Today she'd dressed in a leopard jumpsuit that shouldn't work, but most definitely does. Then again, I don't think there's a single thing Meg could clothe herself with that wouldn't have me licking my lips. The woman's magnetism defies description.

She steps into the room and carefully closes the door behind her. I should say something, should do something, should stop staring and shake off this spell she weaves over me just by existing in the same room. I can't quite manage it. Meg studies me with a small smile pulling at her lips. "Power suits you. I knew it would."

That unsticks me. "You didn't know a single damn thing. You *gave* me to Ali."

She shrugs. "He made a deal. Hades holds my leash, baby girl. Something as simple as friendship doesn't hold a candle."

"Are we friends?" I hate that the question slips free, but it's too late. It floats in the space between us.

She tilts her head to the side. "We could be. In time."

Time for me to forgive. I'm not there yet. I don't care how things turned out, how I handled the situation to land on my feet. She didn't know that would happen when she handed me over. *Hades* didn't know it would happen, either. I doubt he cared one way or another what happened once his side of the deal with fulfilled. "Does he know you're here?"

"Probably." She shrugs a single shoulder. "My tether is long enough when he's in the mood to be generous."

I still can't really wrap my mind around their relationship, which is likely hypocritical. After all, Jafar and I are hardly traditional in any sense of the word. I look to him, trying to understand what he wants to accomplish with this visit. He, even more than I, holds a grudge against what they did. Against what could have happened to me before he got there.

He seems content to let this play out. His relaxed posture is a lie, though. I know him well enough to read the tension in the line of his shoulders and the coldness in his dark eyes as he watches her. If Meg makes one wrong move, he'll haul her out of here. I frown. "If you didn't want her here, why is she my surprise?"

Jafar cuts a look in my direction. "She's not your surprise." Now Meg gets a sharp look. "You don't normally play errand girl."

"I do when the situation calls for it." Under his stare, she wilts the tiniest bit. It lasts for a single breath, too short for me to have noticed if I wasn't watching so closely. Then she lifts her chin, once again standing on solid ground. "I'm here to apologize."

"You're not forgiven," Jafar says.

I fold my arms over my chest and glare. "I can speak for myself, at least in this."

"Would you like me to detail all the harm that could have befallen you in Ali's tender care? I'm more than capable of it, Jasmine. You didn't see the worst he had to offer, and it's a fucking miracle that *you* are responsible for. *They* couldn't have known you would be able to protect yourself." He flings a hand in Meg's direction.

"He's right," she says. "I don't deserve your forgiveness, and I don't expect it, but I'm apologizing all the same."

I'm not ready to forgive.

That's the truth of it. Even if Hades holds Meg's leash, literally or otherwise, she still made a choice to betray me, and it's not something I'll get over anytime soon. And yet... I walk around my desk and lean against it, putting us all on more equal footing. "I'll think about it."

"Thank you." She actually seems like she means it, which is more than I expected. I know better than to trust this contriteness, though. People are more than capable of lying with both their words and their bodies. *I'm* more than capable of it. Meg walks forward and sinks gracefully to her knees in front of me. She gives me a surprisingly sweet smile. "I had fun with you, Jasmine."

My throat suddenly feels too dry. "I had fun with you, too." All too easy to imagine her inching closer and pushing my skirt up and... I give myself a mental shake. She's not here for that, no matter what position she holds at the moment.

Jafar stalks over and leans again the desk next to me. He doesn't quite touch me, but he doesn't have to. His presence grounds me, allowing me to draw in a full breath. He looks down at Meg. "Interesting way of delivery."

"What can I say? I'm a showman at heart." She pulls a large square black velvet box out of her purse and holds up in with both hands. "Your surprise, Jasmine." She opens it and my heart stops.

It's a diamond necklace.

Its design is deceptively simple, a single row of diamonds that meet in the middle with a tail that drapes down to a large ruby at the end of it. It's one of the most beautiful things I've ever seen.

"Do you like it?"

I turn to look at Jafar, frowning at the strange note in his voice. No nerves show on his face, but that earlier tension is back. It's almost as if he's...holding his breath. I focus back on the necklace and the truth rolls over me. It's not a necklace. It's a *collar*.

Not quite a ring, no, but something akin to it. A claim of permanent long-term ownership. Everyone in the Underworld knows that Jafar owns me, that I belong to him and him alone. This is different. People come together and part in the Underworld and then move back into the world without strings attached.

This marks me as Jafar's for people like us, people who will know what it means, outside the club. In public.

"Would you like to put it on?" So careful, my love. Watching me so closely. There are times when he's all too happy to steamroll me—when I'm all too happy to be steamrolled—but this doesn't number among them. This is a step, a serious step, one to be made with eyes wide open.

I should probably make him wait, but I can't quite manage to play that game. "Yes, Daddy."

He picks it up, his gaze not straying from my face, and settles it over my head. The necklace is on a slip knot type thing, and once he adjusts it, he pauses, holding the tail. The ruby shines in his palm and then he releases it to allow it to rest between my breasts. Even though I know it's actually room temperature, I can't help feeling like I've been branded by this necklace. By his touch.

"Get out, Meg."

She rises gracefully to her feet. "Enjoy."

I don't take my eyes from Jafar as Meg leaves the room and closes the door softly behind her. He uses two fingers to lift my chin and drags his thumb over my bottom lip. "You like it."

"I love it." I nip his thumb and am rewarded by heat flaring in his dark eyes. "Thank you, Daddy."

"I want to see you in nothing but the collar."

Another day, I'd push him, mouth off, make him force me. I don't want to play that game today. I step back and unbutton my shirt. My skirt, bra, and panties follow it to the floor in quick succession, until I stand before him naked but for the collar. I've never felt more powerful than in that moment when his breath catches the tiniest bit. He's just as affected as I am by this. Day or night, we're equals now in a way we never quite managed before.

We have a *future* now.

I hold his gaze as I sink to my knees, a silent acknowledgement that I choose this again and again. That I will continue to do so. That I choose *him*.

Jafar regards me for a long moment, the silence filled

with countless possibilities. I can see the exact moment he settles on one. He bends down and catches me under my arms, hauling me to my feet. "You should let Meg make it up to you."

"I'll forgive her when I'm ready," I snap. He can dictate so many things in our private lives, but not *this*. "And I don't know why you're bothering to advocate on her behalf. You're even more furious at her than I am."

"Yes, I am." He considers me for a long moment. "Don't move."

"Jafar—" It's too late. He's gone, disappearing through the door and leaving me standing in my study wearing nothing but my collar. I want to storm after him, to tell him that I don't need him controlling *this* the same way he controls so much else. But part of me wants to know what his plans are.

He doesn't make me wait long. Two minutes later, he walks back into the room with Meg on his heels. Jafar snaps his fingers at her. "Kneel."

I expect her to snap back. The only other time we did this, Meg was definitely in a dominant position, despite Jafar holding the reins. She doesn't, though. She simply obeys. Only then does Jafar move to the chaise lounge chair I have positioned in front of the large windows overlooking the terrace garden. It's one of my favorite features of this study. He sinks onto the chaise and crooks his fingers at me. "Come here, baby girl."

I skirt around Meg and walk to him. He positions me next to him and drapes an arm over the back of the chaise, giving all the appearance of being at ease. "You have penance to enact, Megaera."

"Yes." She doesn't lift her eyes.

For the first time, I wonder if she's truly as sorry as she

said she was. If maybe she's just as caught up in this mess as everyone else is. Is she innocent? Not by a long shot. But we all operate in cages, whether they're of our own making or someone else's. Perhaps she really did feel the same connection I did. Something more than friendship, but significantly less than what I feel for Jafar.

He twines a lock of my hair around his finger. "You know how to make it up to her."

"I do." She crawls to me. It's not like last time, where she was all power and predatory lines. Meg crawls to me like a true submissive. Graceful, yes, but it's not the same at all. I don't know how to feel about this.

Jafar doesn't give me a chance to consider it. He hitches one of my legs over his lap, opening me for her. "Make it good, Meg. This is the first of many. You can't earn her forgiveness, but you can certainly weigh the balance in your favor."

I shoot him a sharp look. "You can't negotiate that on my behalf."

"No, I can't." He brings one of my hands to his mouth and kisses my knuckles, devastatingly gentle. "But if I want to see you come on Meg's face, that's exactly what you're going to do, baby girl."

"I—" The first drag of Meg's tongue steals my words. I melt back against Jafar, letting his strength steady me as Meg grips my thighs and licks my pussy as if she can find the penance she's looking for there. As if she truly can earn it.

Jafar shifts, sliding one arm behind my back so he can hold me. He pinches my nipple, the sharp pain making me gasp. "You're teasing her, Meg." The censor in his tone makes me shake in the most delicious way possible. Jafar reaches down with his free hand and laces his fingers through her mass of dark hair. "Lick her here." He guides her up to my clit. "Stop fucking around."

Meg stops fucking around. She sucks my clit hard and pushes two fingers into me. I try to resist, to hold out, but it's too much. My back bows and I cry out as my orgasm rolls over me. I slump back against Jafar, dazed and yet wanting more.

I always want more.

He uses his grip on Meg's hair to lift her head. "That's a start."

She licks her lips and gives a faint smile. "It's a long path to redemption. At least this one is pleasurable." She reaches up and cups my chin briefly. "I truly am sorry, Jasmine." She rises and walks out of the room, and this time she doesn't come back.

I crawl into Jafar's lap and he obliges me by holding me close. "I'll forgive her eventually."

"I know."

"Does that make me weak?" She betrayed me. I should be ready to go after her with everything I can bring to the fore. Instead, I'm just tired. There are plenty of fights left in my future. If I can let this go...

I will. Not today. But eventually.

I lift my face and kiss Jafar. "Thank you."

"I'll always give you what you need, baby girl. Always."

THIS SHORT ORIGINALLY APPEARED AS the July 2019 short for my Patreon. Each month, patrons nominate their favorite couples and characters, vote on one, and I write a brand new short featuring the winner. For more bonus stories, please consider joining my Patreon.

JASMINE'S WINTER SOLSTICE
JASMINE

I never imagined I'd love the politics that go with running my own territory. The power? Yes, of course I want that. I've had a taste, and I'll never go back to being the girl who was more pawn than human.

But there's something about communicating in dual meanings that appeals to me. A statement that seems benign, but holds a multitude of threats beneath the surface. A compliment that's actually anything but. I thrive in this constant battle with words and edged smiles and body language.

Tonight is one such occasion.

I look around the ballroom. My generals and their partners mingle with Jafar's men. Even after nearly a year, the tension is thick enough to drown in. They don't trust each other, and I haven't bothered to change that. More than half of these people supported Jafar's coup against my father. They are not my friends, and they are not to be trusted. They are, however, incredibly useful now that I've unlocked the key.

Still, after hours of this song and dance, weariness

weighs me down. I want eight hours of sleep, a bath, and Jafar; not necessarily in that order.

As if my thoughts summon the man himself, he emerges from a cluster of men in suits and stalks in my direction. I let myself look my fill. He's putting on this show for me, after all. And it's *quite* the show, even if it might not appear to be from the outside. Even after months and months together, this man still takes my breath away. He wears a charcoal suit with a dark purple shirt that sets off his medium-brown skin to perfection. Each movement is full of promise of things to come. A promise echoed in his dark eyes.

He reaches me and turns easily to take up his position at my right shoulder, nearly close enough to touch. His low voice reaches me easily despite the relative din of conversation filling the room. "You've done well."

The praise warms me, but I keep my expression cool. "I know."

A small smile touches his lips. "Meet me in the gazebo in an hour. This lot will have cleared out by then."

That's an ambitious timeline. It's barely eleven, and the last time I threw a party like this, nearly every person stayed until the sun rose the next day. Not all of them were conscious at that point, but they were bodily present. "You may be waiting in the gazebo a long time."

He just smiles and walks away. His smugness is irritating in the extreme, as is his ability to move freely around during these events. I'm stuck in what's essentially a throne, surveying my kingdom. Most of the time I enjoy these little power plays, the way I can use my position within a room to illustrate that I'm the one to answer to.

Not tonight.

Tonight, my exhaustion goes bone deep.

It would be an unforgivable reach to call my late father a

sentimental man. He barely made time to be my jailer, let alone an actual father. I hated him as much as I loved him—more, even. But, every winter solstice, we would walk the gardens together. First the greenhouses, then the ones outside that went dormant with the turning of the year. A way of remembering my mother, though sometimes I wonder if my memories are true or just figments of my yearning for something *else*.

I never thought to miss him. I certainly never considered that his loss would compound my lack of mother. Grief works in strange ways, I suppose. My father was a terrible man. He locked me in a cage, had fully intended to barter me for his own personal gain, neglected and abused me in turn. I *hate* that I miss him at times. Just a little, a flicker of loss in an otherwise wonderful life.

Tonight, on the winter solstice, the flicker is stronger than it's ever been.

The exodus to the entrance starts so slowly, I barely notice it at first. But as my generals approach me, one by one, to say their goodbyes, and I realize Jafar must be responsible for this. My chest warms the tiniest bit. He and I haven't spoken about what this time of year means to me, but obviously he sensed my disquiet as the day approached.

Exactly fifty minutes after Jafar gave his order, the room is clear but for his people. I slip out the door and head for the back entrance of the house that leads into the gardens and the massive maze that stretches over several acres. My sanctuary for so many years.

It started snowing sometime after sunset, and a light layer of white coats the path and dusts the slumbering plants. I tilt my head back and take my first true breath in hours, letting the frigid air coat my lungs and clear my thoughts.

My feet know the path, even if I haven't been out here much since I gained leadership of this territory. It took six months to stabilize things after the coup and subsequent second coup. Even now, when things are mostly running smoothly, there's no *time*. My days are filled with numbers and negotiations and politics.

I love it. I truly do. Tomorrow, I'll love it even more.

Tonight, I'm simply tired.

The gazebo is tucked back in the maze. Not the center, but in one of the four courtyards scattered throughout the bending paths. I've spent nearly as many hours in this maze as I have in the house itself. It's child's play to craft my route, and I don't make a single wrong turn.

I step into the courtyard at exactly the hour mark and stop short. I'm not certain what I expected, but the gazebo is swathed in darkness. A thrill of fear goes through me and I savor it the same way I savored the expensive wine I drank earlier. "Jafar?"

A whisper of sound behind me. I barely have a moment to brace before he catches my hips and hauls me back against his body. "Tell me your safe word, baby girl."

My answer is immediate and breathy. "Rajah."

"I'm feeling generous tonight, so I'll let you tell me what you need." He drags his mouth down my neck. "We can go into the gazebo, and I can take care of you nice and slow." He grins against my skin. "Or I can chase you through the maze."

I lean back against him, seeking the strength of his solidness. "Do you fancy yourself the Minotaur, Daddy?"

"I'm going to do significantly more than eat you when I catch you."

I shiver. "Chase me."

I expect him to give me a little push, to send me on my

way with a count ringing in my ears. I should know better by now. Jafar turns me around and goes easily to his knees before me. "Brace yourself on my shoulders."

Before I can ask him what the hell he's doing, he takes my ankle and unbuckles the little strap holding my heel in place. Cold bites at my bare foot as he repeats the process with the other.

He answers my unspoken question without looking up. "I'm not having this night end with you twisting an ankle."

I don't bother to argue that I could run a 5k in heels if I so chose. These paths are slippery and the snow makes it impossible to gauge the dips and unevenness of the ground. "Just a little frostbite, then?"

"You won't evade me long enough to get frostbite, baby girl." The heavy threat in his voice has my entire body responding. We haven't played like this in a long time. The house is never empty, and a quick chase around the bedroom isn't anything compared to what he's offering me tonight.

What he offered me the first time we were together.

I can't quite remove the shakiness from my voice when I say, "You'll never catch me."

"Would you like to bet on that?" He rises easily to his feet. The moon is barely a crescent in the sky, and the darkness hides his expression from me, turning him into something dangerous and forbidden. "If you make it to the maze entrance—"

"I want to watch you fuck Alaric." Since our initial trip to the Underworld, I've become quite familiar with Hades's staff. Alaric is a switch who's pretty enough to turn even me into a fumbling mess. I got over that reaction quickly, and now I can see him without making a fool of myself. Mostly.

Jafar's grip tightens on my hips ever so slightly. "You've

been ruminating on that fantasy for quite some time if you're able to rattle it off without hesitation."

There's no point in denying it. "Yes."

"Very well. If you make it to the maze entrance, I will put on a show for you with Alaric." He grins, a flash of teeth in the meager moonlight. "And if you don't make it, you'll take a week off."

I blink. Of all the things I expected him to say, this didn't number among them. "What?"

"An entire week. Seven days. We will go somewhere that isn't Carver City, and you will not take any communication for the duration."

The prospect both thrills me and makes me vaguely sick to my stomach. "That's impossible. What if something happens while we're gone and we're needed back here immediately? What if someone stages yet another coup and—"

"Those are the terms, baby girl. Take them or leave them."

I narrow my eyes. "You're such an asshole." When he doesn't respond, apparently content to wait me out, I sigh. "Fine. I agree."

He leans down and brushes his lips against the shell of my ear. "You have to the count of five."

"*Five?* What the hell, Jafar?"

"Five." He shrugs out of his jacket and moves to the gazebo to drape it over the railing. "Four."

I take off running, my bare feet hitting the cold ground, each impact a shock to my system. I'd had half a mind to let him catch me before he laid out the terms. Now, I simply cannot allow it.

"One." His voice echoes through the maze, and I pick up speed. My instincts overtake my rational thinking. This is not a game between willing prey and a loving predator. This is a pursuit I might not recover from. Fear clogs my throat, my breath heavy in my lungs. My mind blanks and I give myself over to the familiar steps.

Left. Left. Right. Left again.

He's chosen his starting point well. With him blocking the most direct route out of the maze, I have to go through the center and out the other side to escape. The turns bleed into one another. I can't hear anything over my harsh breathing, can't tell if he's closing in, can't do anything but flee mindlessly, a fox before the hound.

I make it two steps into the center of the maze. Two momentous steps when I think I might be able to do this, to escape.

Jafar catches me around the waist and hauls me to the ground. I don't miss the fact that I've landed on grass instead of the path, and I certainly don't miss the fact that his hand cradles my head to ensure it doesn't make contact. Even knowing that, knowing that I'm with someone I trust implicitly, I still fight. "Let me go!"

"You know better." He pins my flailing hands over my head and transfers them to one hand. "You're mine to do with as I wish."

I try to kick at him, but my dress hampers my movements. For a moment, I think it might hamper his intentions too, but there's a rip and the cold lashes me from the waist down. He just tore my fucking dress. I thrash harder. "You bastard!"

"Yes." He drags off my panties, easily overpowering me, moving my body to his whim despite my determination not to make this easy for him. And then his hand is there, palming my pussy, claiming me as his own. "Your body always betrays you, baby girl. No matter how much you scream 'no,' you're fighting yourself not to fuck my fingers right now."

I hate that he's right.

I love that he's right.

I'm torn between spreading my legs for him and trying to kick him in the balls. I twist my hips, trying to dislodge him. It doesn't work. Of course it doesn't work.

Jafar covers me with his body, but he's not lining up with where I need him. He presses me down to the cold ground, his hand between my legs, and pushes a single finger into me. "I'll always give you what you need, baby girl. Even when you're too stubborn to ask for it."

"I don't want this." The lie is all part of the game, but my brain gets things all tangled up. I don't *want* a vacation. I don't want time to think, to feel the things weighing on me.

"Maybe not." He fucks me slowly with that finger. Taunting me with my helplessness. Taunting me with my wanton desire. "But you need this."

I'm still forming my denial when he moves. He flips me onto my stomach and rips the skirt of the dress the rest of the way off. I spare a thought to how pissed Tink will be when she finds out what happened to all her hard work, but then Jafar's hauling me to my hands and knees and there's no room for anything else.

He doesn't give me time to brace, and when he shoves his cock deep, I nearly smash my face into the frozen grass. Only his rough hold on my shoulder, pinning me to his cock, saves me.

Then there's no more space for words, for denial. There is only fucking, harsh and primal and rough enough that I'll have bruises in the morning. I'll relish them, just like I'll relish the grass stains on my palms and knees.

Jafar fucks me like he wants to imprint himself on my

very soul. Harsh, deep strokes, yanking me back onto his cock as he shoves forward. Each one drives a helpless sound from my throat. I've forgotten the game, forgotten that I'm supposed to be fighting this. I can only feel.

He shifts his grip, sliding his hand from my hip to my clit. The shock of cold from his fingers makes me gasp. "Now, my little slut." He does something with his hips that change the angle, until he's grinding against my G-stop as he circles my clit. "Scream my name when you come so everyone knows it's my cock you crave."

"Fuck you," I gasp, even as I know I'll do exactly that. He makes me feel so dirty and so protected, all at the same time. I love it. I love *him*.

And then there's no more space for fighting. My body takes over and I'm coming. I dig my fingers into the cold earth and scream Jafar's name as my orgasm rolls through me with the strength of a tidal wave. Through it all, he keeps fucking me, keeps drawing the waves higher and higher until my arms give out and it's only his hold that keeps me off the ground.

I'm vaguely aware of Jafar lifting me into his arms and carrying me through the maze back to the courtyard with the gazebo. I expect him to take me back to the house, but he moves into the gazebo itself. Warmth licks my bare skin and I lift my head enough to see that there's a space heater and a pile of blankets. "What's this?"

"Shhh." He lowers us to the floor and strips me out of the remains of my dress. Even with the space heater, it's chilly, so I'm grateful when he wraps one of the blankets around my body and shifts me to straddle him.

I'm already reaching for the front of his pants and withdrawing his still-hard cock. Even with desire buzzing in my veins, I feel clear-headed for the first time in days. "Thank you."

His hands settle on my hips as I sink onto his cock. "I'll always give you what you need, baby girl." His voice goes a little rough. "And if you wanted to watch me fuck Alaric, all you had to do is ask."

"I want to watch you fuck Alaric, Daddy." I rock my hips, taking him deeper, even as I spill this fantasy into the darkness between us. "I like that you let others play with me. A lot. But I want to watch him suck your cock, and then I want to watch you fuck his ass."

"Mmm." He nips my bottom lip. "You'll sit there with your hand up your short little skirt and finger yourself while I do."

"Yes, Daddy." I wrap the blanket around his shoulders too, encasing us in a cozy warmth. In our own little world. I ride his cock in slow strokes, drawing out the dreamlike quality this night has taken. This is the come-down from the chase, the slow ascension of pleasure, the feeling of him so close to me in every way that counts. There are times when I love being naked while he's clothed, but I suddenly need skin to skin.

I reach for his buttons with trembling fingers, but he anticipates me, brushing my hands away so he can make quick work of them. Jafar hooks an arm around my waist and rolls us. Some creative disrobing and then he's as naked as I am. I wrap my legs around his hips and my arms around his back.

This. This right here is what I need. Different from before, but no less valued for it.

I want this to last forever, but all too soon my body takes the choice from me. I press my face to his shoulder as I come, clinging to him. This time, Jafar follows me over the edge.

He rolls slightly to the side and drags a blanket over us. I rest my head on his chest, holding him tightly as our hearts slow and the sweat cools on our bodies. Finally, I lift my head and frown at him. "A vacation? *Really?*"

"Yes."

I wait, but he doesn't seem interested in offering more explanation. "But why?"

"As I said before, time and time again." He brushes his thumb across my bottom lip. "I'll always give you what you need. Even if you fight me every step of the way."

"I like fighting you," I respond automatically, but my mind is whirling. I didn't realize how the walls were starting to feel like they're closing in until he offers me a reprieve. "You've already got this planned out, haven't you?"

"We fly out in the morning."

I stare. "What would have happened if I made it to the maze entrance and ruined all your plans?"

His dark laugh has my body clenching despite several delicious orgasms. "You were never making it to the maze entrance and we both know it."

I suppose we do.

We lay like that for a long time, but Jafar finally urges me up. I'm still dreading the naked trek back to the house when he pulls out a bag tucked back behind the space heater and proceeds to dress me in leggings, a thick knitted sweater, socks, and boots. A hat and jacket finish the outfit. I look down at myself and then at him. "What is this?"

He pulls his own clothes back on quickly and shuts off the space heater. "It's the winter solstice."

"Yes," I say slowly.

Jafar gives me a look. Even without much light, I can feel

the censor in it. "Come now, Jasmine. You can't think I've forgotten your tradition."

I should have known. I should have known he'd notice and catalogue it away in that impressively twisty brain of his. *Of course* he realized, even before I did, that this was something I needed. "Thank you," I whisper.

Jafar tucks my hand into the crook of his arm and we walk together out of the maze. Instead of turning toward the house, we move to the gardens. It's almost the opposite route of the one I always took with my father, but that feels good and right.

A new tradition, built on the old, but different.

Perfect.

3

A PROPOSAL

I am so tired. The kind of exhaustion that settles in my bones to stay. It has nothing to do with the amount of sleep I achieve each night and everything to do with the sheer stress that comes from running a territory. From being a woman running a territory that's had a man at the helm for decades.

I rub the bridge of my nose, careful not to touch my eyes and smudge my makeup. I've had to make examples of people. To do things that feed my nightmares that same way Ali's death lingers in that darkest recesses of my soul.

I feel Jafar before I see him. It's as if the very air in the room shifts to accommodate his presence. He's always been like that, but the longer we've been together the more attuned to him I become.

He stops behind me and then his hands are on my shoulders, thumbs digging into the tight muscles there. "We're done for the day."

"I have one more meeting." A video call with the newest territory head—Cordelia. I feel a foolish sort of kinship with her, another daughter stepping into the larger-than-life shoes of her deceased father. I won't let that kinship muddy the waters when our territories share a border, but I can't deny it. "I can't put it off. It's Cordelia Belmont."

"You're right. You can't put it off." He finds a knot and digs his thumb in hard enough to buckle my knees and make me moan a little. "Do you need me?"

I smile. "Always."

"Baby girl."

I turn in his arms and slide my hands up his chest. "After this, I'm going to be too wound up to sleep."

His lips curve. "That wasn't even a subtle hint."

"No, it wasn't." I press a quick kiss to his lips, barely resisting the urge to sink into it. I don't have time. There's never enough time anymore. Someone always needs something from me, and nights are my only relief, the only time I can let down my walls and just be *me* with Jafar. The moment I walk through the doors of our suite and kick off my heels always feels like taking off a corset after wearing it for hours upon hours.

He sets me back and strokes his hands down my arms. "You have this under control. Cordelia isn't in a position to press us, not when she has Ursa biting at her heels on the other side."

"Jafar." I wait for him to look at me. "I know. I have access to the same information you do."

He laughs softly. "Sometimes it's hard taking a backseat in these meetings and negotiations."

"I can't imagine why." I arch my brows. "You aren't staging another coup, are you?"

"When the last one went so well?" He takes my hand, his finger brushing my bare left ring finger. He's been patient, but in the last month or so, he's been touching me there more and more often. I suspect he'd want his ring on my finger no matter what, but after the unconventional offering in marriage I got from Abel Paine a few weeks ago, Jafar has been more subtly possessive. "They won't stop asking, you know."

Of course his mind's gone to the same place mine has. I glance at the clock, but I still have a few minutes. "Jafar, he literally gave me a pick of his six brothers to marry, sight unseen. That's hardly a tempting offer." I step to him, pressing myself against his chest. "*No one* is as tempting as you, Daddy."

He sets his hands on my hips, but the dark emotions don't fade from his eyes. "I'll wait as long as you need." He urges me closer, rolling my hips against his hardening cock. "But some day, I want my ring on your finger, baby girl. I thought I could give it up, but that was before."

I'm not really opposed to the idea. Once people stop looking at me and seeing weakness because of my gender, marrying Jafar will carry less risk of undermining my position. I wish it wasn't something I had to consider, wish our happiness didn't rank lower than the lives of everyone in our territory, but life is full of hard choices. "I love you."

"I love you, too." He turns me around and gives me a little nudge. "You're going to be late."

I wish I didn't have to push pause on this conversation, but showing up late for this meeting isn't an option. I barely make it to my chair in time to pull up the appropriate link and dial in. Cordelia's pretty face appears almost instantly, her dark hair pulled back and her expression serious. "Hello, Jasmine."

"Cordelia."

We verbally spar for a few moments and then get down to business, but half my mind lingers at how uneasy Jafar looked. It wouldn't be obvious to someone who didn't know him well, but I've spent a lifetime studying that man's expressions and I know his face almost as well as my own. Something's bothering him, and I can't begin to guess if it's the lack of marriage or something else entirely.

By the time I finish with the call with Cordelia, neither of us have made much in the way of promises. We're in an uneasy truce that I don't trust her to honor any more than she trusts me. I expect there will extra eyes on the border on both sides, but only time will prove if we're as good as our word. I know *I* am, but she's even newer to this. If she's smart, she'll focus on transitioning her people's loyalty to her before she makes any big moves against her neighbors —and hopefully *never* makes big moves. Peace between factions is profitable for everyone. Most of Carver City's territory leaders recognize that, but as the two newest ones, Cordelia and I are the ones everyone is watching to see if we'll rock the boat. I have no intention of doing it. Cordelia claims the same.

We'll see.

I stand and stretch. Jafar has long since disappeared, and I head out of my study and through the halls. After much arguing, Jafar and I compromised by having men stationed on the main floor in key spots but leaving the second floor to us alone. I see a few of them as I head to the stairs, and nod in acknowledgement. It's hard to keep yourself regal and distant when your feet are screaming and your back hurts and there's a headache starting behind one eye. But then, I've had months of practice at this point.

I don't breathe easy until I close the door of our personal

suite and lean against it. One of the first things I did upon taking control of this house and this territory was to have one of the spare suites renovated to fit out needs. Staying in my room felt too strange. Moving into my father's suite? Unthinkable.

I actually moan as I kick off my heels. I love them. I do. But after long days, it's more of a love-hate relationship.

"Baby girl."

Just like that, the worst of my exhaustion slides right off me. I push off the door and move further into the suite. "Daddy, I'm home."

His dark laugh comes from the direction of the bathroom. Curious, I follow the sound and stop just inside the doorway. This bathroom is one of my favorite parts of the house now. It's all done up in dark slate gray tile, with a massive claw-foot bathtub that is ridiculous and extravagant and I love with all my heart. Right now, it's filled with steaming water. "What's all this?"

"You've had a long day."

"Every day is a long day right now. For both of us."

"Mmm." Jafar crooks his finger at me. "Come here."

I couldn't disobey that quiet command if I wanted to, and I desperately don't want to. I walk to him and slip my hand into his. He uses that touch to turn me to face away from him, and then unzips my dress. Jafar kisses my neck as he eases the fabric off my body. "Did you eat lunch today?"

"Yes, Daddy." I smile a little. "Impossible not to when you order the chef to deliver it at noon, regardless of where I am or what I'm doing." Initially, I'd chafed at that little display of dominance, but it's simply Jafar taking care of me. If left to my own devices, we both know I'd work through lunch more often than I'd remember to eat it.

"Dinner?"

"Not yet."

"Thought so." He twists my hair up on top of my head and fastens it there. "In the bath. You need it."

I really, really do need it, but I can't help poking at him a little. "Are you saying I stink?"

"Baby girl, if you want to play the brat, this night is going to go significantly different than I'd planned."

I almost push him further. I love it when my man snaps, when we play rough. But tonight? I don't know if I'm up for it. "Yes, Daddy." I manage to sound suitably meek. I think.

His low chuckle makes my entire body clench. "In."

I climb into the tub. It's built big enough for both of us, so I'm practically swimming in it. I lean my head back against the rim and watch him. "What do you have planned for us tonight?"

Jafar leans against the counter. He's still wearing his black slacks and a pinstriped button-down shirt that looks particularly delicious. But what really gets me is that he's barefoot. I don't know that I'll ever get used to the fact that this man is *mine*, that he lets down his walls around me and no one else. It's a shared privilege, but no less novel for it.

Finally, he moves, unbuttoning his shirt with little flicks of his fingers. It comes off and he drapes it over the back of the chair arranged next to the tub. His pants are next, and then he's naked and moving to climb into the bath and settle behind me. His sigh tells me everything I need to know.

I shift to settle my head against his shoulder and wrap his arms around me. "It's been a long day for both of us."

"A long week."

I smile. "A long month, quarter, year."

Jafar chuckles. "Yes." He gives me a squeeze.

Maybe I should leave things at that, but our earlier

conversation still lingers. I turn and carefully straddle him. "I do want to marry you, you know."

Just like that, his expression closes down. "We've talked about this. I know your reasons for holding off. They're good ones."

"Just because they're good ones doesn't mean we should ignore the elephant in the room." I drape my arms around his neck and sift my fingers through his hair. It's getting longer; he'll need a cut soon. "Jafar, you're the only one for me. Just you. I've been more than a little in love with you since long before you ever fucked me in the middle of my father's hallway."

His expression stays closed down, but there's a wicked glint in his eye. "I know."

"Then what's this about? You know I'm yours. A ring is just..." I trail off, understanding dawning. "It's not about us, is it? It's about everyone else."

He looks away, the barest movement that's almost a flinch. "Everyone who matters in Carver City knows that we're together. It never occurred to me that I'd have to worry about people in other cities looking at you as a tempting fruit to pick."

I settle more firmly against him. "Jafar, I'm no one's fruit. Not even yours."

"I know that. They don't."

I lean down and kiss his neck. Even though he stays tense beneath me, his cock hardens. "Would it make you feel better to tattoo your name on my ass?"

"No one can see a tattoo like that. I won't serve the same purpose." Finally, *finally*, his voice thaws. "Are you offering, baby girl?"

"Nope." I nip him and shift, sliding my breasts against his chest. "It was a purely theoretical question."

He's silent for several long moments even as I move against him and his hands slide down to my ass to urge me not to stop. Finally, he says, "It bothered me. That Paine thought he could come in here and you'd let him or one of his brothers in willingly."

"Is that what bothered you?" I reach between us and guide his cock into me. It's not as smooth as normal, not with the water encompassing us, but it's worth it when he's finally sheathed to the hilt inside me. I rock my hips a little. "Or is it the fact that he didn't look at you once the entire time he was here?"

"Baby girl," his voice is low. Warning me.

As if I don't love provoking him as much as he loves being provoked. I lean back a little and make a show of biting my bottom lip. "Is that why you fucked me on my desk the second he left the grounds? Were you feeling threatened, Daddy?"

He makes a sound suspiciously like a growl. "You're mine, Jasmine. And I'm yours. That smug bastard thought I wasn't even a threat to his plans."

"And yet it's *your* cock I'm riding right now."

"Yes. It is." He loops an arm around my waist and stands. I have to cling to him as he steps out of the bath and walks us out into the bedroom.

"Jafar, I'm all wet!"

"We'll change the bedding." He climbs onto the mattress and bears us both down. But he doesn't start fucking me like I expect. He just looks down at me, at my body, at the spot where we're joined. "Promise me that someday you'll say yes."

I'm already nodding. "I will. I promise that someday I'll say yes."

He's still for so long, I almost wonder if he doesn't

believe me. But then it's like something snaps in him. He presses me into the mattress and starts to fuck me so roughly, I have to slam my hands to the headboard to keep myself in place. It's like he's trying to imprint himself on every inch of me.

This isn't about me at all. It's about Jafar.

And that's why I release the headboard and wrap myself around him. "I love you. I'm yours, Daddy. Just yours."

He finally buries his face in my neck and goes still. For half a second, I think he's orgasmed, but he slowly starts moving again. "I'm not taking care of you," he murmurs against my skin.

"I like everything you do to me. Even when I hate it."

His laugh makes me moan. Finally Jafar props himself up on his elbows and looks down at me. "I'll never admit to insecurity. But if I were a man who'd admit as much, it's possible that Abel Paine made me feel it... and jealous."

I nod solemnly. "I'm shocked to learn that you're actually human. Very, very shocked."

"Brat."

"Yes." I wiggle a little. "I suppose you should do something about that."

His expression goes downright forbidding. "I suppose I should." He pulls out of me and then he's hauling me up and over his lap and delivering a stinging slap to my ass. "Bad girls get spanked. Isn't that right, baby girl?"

"Yes, Daddy! I'm sorry, Daddy!" I apologize even as I arch back to take the next strike.

This is perfection. This is exactly what I need, what we both need. This is *us*.

When Jafar finally stops spanking me, my ass is on fire and I'm practically begging for his cock again. This time, when he drives into me, he's holding me just as close as I'm holding him. He's here with me, not driving away the fear of me leaving him.

When we finally exhaust ourselves, he changes the bedding and tucks us in together. I snuggle up against his chest and hook my leg over his hips. "Jafar, I have a question."

"Mmmm?" He sifts his fingers through my hair.

I lift myself up enough to see his face. "Will you marry me?"

He goes stock still. "Don't toy with me, Jasmine."

"I mean it." I let him see the truth on my face. This isn't a joke, isn't a bratting thing. It's earnest. "It's been over a year. I... I thought I wanted to wait, but you're right. There's always going to be some new challenge, someone looking to capitalize on my position. There's no reason to wait. I love you. I want you to be my husband."

Jafar shifts to the side and pulls open the nightstand. He lifts out a square black box. "You know, I had intended to plan something special when you finally said you were ready."

"Sorry?"

"I'm not." He opens the box and reveals a ring with a massive ruby framed by diamonds. "It made me think of you."

"It's perfect," I breathe.

He slides it onto my finger and, of course, it fits just as perfectly. Jafar rolls me onto my back and kisses me. "Jasmine. Baby girl. *Wife*." Another kiss. "I love you."

"I love you, too." I dig my hands into his hair and tow him back to my mouth. "Forever, Jafar."

"Forever."

∾

THIS SHORT ORIGINALLY APPEARED AS the May 2020 short for my Patreon. Each month, patrons nominate their favorite couples and characters, vote on one, and I write a brand new short featuring the winner. For more bonus stories, please consider joining my Patreon.

4

GOING PUBLIC, PART 1

MEG

"People don't celebrate one month anniversaries."

Hades gives me a look that statement no doubt deserves. "You're arguing just for the sake of arguing, love."

He's not wrong. The last four weeks with Hades and Hercules have been a whirlwind of bliss. Even as a rational part of my mind tries to convince me that we're simply in the honeymoon stage, that reality will filter in at some point, it never quite gains traction. I'm too damn happy to poke holes in our relationship. It's almost a relief to realize it. I don't *have* to pick things apart. Challenges will arise, but we'll deal with them just like we dealt with the hurdles at the beginning.

I shiver as Hercules runs his fingers through my hair and presses them against my temples, massaging gently. I'm sitting between his thighs on the bed as we watch Hades get dressed. He has a meeting this morning with Isabelle Belmonte, the youngest daughter of the Man in Black. I'm very curious to hear what's brought her here. She and her sisters never visit the Underworld, but that doesn't stop the rumor mill from churning, especially when this is the woman who led both Beast and Gaeton around by their cocks before dumping them and escalating their rivalry into true enmity.

Or that's how the story goes. Only those three know the full truth.

Those three and perhaps Hades.

Hercules moves to the tense spots at the base of my skull and I can't hold back a little moan. He chuckles. "Let us have our fun, Meg."

As if I would tell them no. Not about something like this, a small celebration of how right things are finally going for us. More, it's an official statement of our relationship to the rest of Carver City. Everyone knows we're together. Tonight will inform them that we are permanent.

I relax back into Hercules and fight to open my eyes. "A public scene."

"Mmm." Hades finishes buttoning his shirt and picks up his jacket. "It's time to let our world know Hercules is ours in truth."

"I suppose if we're going to celebrate a made-up anniversary, this is an excellent way to go about it."

"I suspected you'd see things our way." He crosses to the bed and presses a quick kiss to my mouth and then does the same to Hercules. "No fucking, you two. I want you fresh tonight." And then he's gone, leaving the suite and us to our own devices.

Hercules loops an arm around my waist and hauls me back into his lap. He sets his teeth against the sensitive spot where my neck meets my shoulder. "Thank you."

"You both knew I was going to say yes."

"Yep." He hooks my thigh and guides my legs wide over his. "Didn't have a single doubt."

"Uh huh." I press my lips together as he cups my pussy and presses two fingers into me. "You're being disobedient."

"Am I?" He chuckles against my skin as he slowly fucks me with his fingers. "He said no fucking. I'm keeping my cock to myself."

I lift my hips to guide him deeper. "You're not obeying the spirit of the command."

"I know." He grinds the heel of his palm against my clit. His voice has gone low and delicious the way it always does when he's turned on. "Do you want me to stop?"

"Yes."

Instantly he removes his hand. I don't give him a chance to apologize. I don't want it. Instead I turn in his arms and push him flat onto the bed. "I don't want to come on your fingers, dirty boy. I want to come all over your face."

The grin he gives me has my heart doing a happy shimmy. I can't help but grin right back. Hercules catches my hips and hauls me up until I'm straddling his head. "Now who's not obeying the spirit of the command?"

"Me." I smack his hands away and turn around. "I want your cock in my mouth while you fuck me with your tongue." I stretch myself over him and take his cock in my hand. "If I come before you do, I'll get out the strap-on for tonight's show." I stroke him slowly as he takes a hold of my thighs and rearranges me for better access. "Would you like me to fuck your ass while the whole of the Underworld watches?"

"Yes," he breathes against my clit.

"Prove it."

I suck him down at the same time that he spreads me

wider yet and drags his tongue over me. I moan. It's always so fucking *good* when Hercules goes down on me. He loves it even more than I do, which only makes it hotter.

The door opens and we both freeze.

Hades tsks softly, his hands in his pockets. "I've been gone thirty seconds."

Answering would require taking Hercules's cock out of my mouth, and I'm not quite willing to do that. I suck him down again, holding Hades's dark gaze. Taunting him. Hercules's hands shake on my thighs, his breath harsh against my clit though he doesn't resume licking me. "Sorry," he manages.

"No, you're not." He walks slowly to the side of the bed. "But you will be tonight." He runs his hands along my bare back, one coming to rest at the base of my skull, the other on my ass. "I suppose there's a reward if you make her come first."

He knows me too well. I try to rise off Hercules's cock, but Hades easily holds me in place. Hercules answer, his voice strained. "She'll use the strap-on on me tonight."

Hades tsks again. "Now you've tied my hands, love. You know how much I enjoy watching you take his ass." He forces me down another inch, damn near gagging me on Hercules's cock. I love it. "Resume, little Hercules. Make her come so hard she chokes on your cock."

"Yes, sir," Hercules growls.

"Ah. A moment." Hades shifts his grip on my ass, sliding his hand down to shove two fingers into me. "So wet, my Meg. So wanton for everything we give you." He withdraws and moves up to my ass, carefully pressing one finger deep. I moan and writhe. It's nowhere near enough, but the penetration holds me pinned in the most delicious way. "*Now* you may begin again."

I try to focus on sucking Hercules's cock, to do what I know will bring him to orgasm. An impossible feat. I can't move with Hades holding me down. I can't do more than cling to Hercules's hips and take what they're giving to me.

Pleasure builds in building waves, crashing through me to the rhythm of Hercules's mouth. I moan and writhe as much as I'm able, but not being only to move freely only makes it hotter.

I don't stand a chance.

I come with a cry and gag, and then Hades is pulling me off Hercules and holding me against him, one finger still in my ass as he uses his free hand to fuck my pussy. I come again, this one lifting me higher yet.

He lays me down next to Hercules, who cuddles me tight against his side. I look down his body as Hades fists his cock. "I'm inclined to reward you obeying *this* command, despite your not honoring the last one."

"Sorry, sir," Hercules says again. He doesn't sound any more sincere this time. He's turning into quite the brat.

I love it. I love him. I stretch up and kiss him, and moan at the taste of myself on his tongue. It would be the simplest thing in the world to sling my leg over Hercules, shift my hips, and take him deep. I might even incite Hades enough to forget he wants to punish us and take my ass. I shiver and start to move.

Hades swats my ass. "You've got your orgasm, love. Two of them, if I don't miss my count. Don't be greedy or I'll be forced to toss you in a cold shower." He'll do it, too. He has before, and no doubt he'll do it again. It's not my fault. I can't get enough of either one of these men. Hades shifts. "Hercules."

Hercules grips my hair with one hand and pulls me away from him a little. "Sorry, Meg."

I grin. "You're about to have Hades's mouth around your cock, so I don't think you're *that* sorry."

"Guilty." He curses and I look down his body to find Hades taking him deep, his dark eyes watching us both. He doesn't tease Hercules. No, he masters his body with a precision that leaves me breathless. I go hot and melty as Hercules's hips jerk before Hades holds him down, forcing him still even as he drives him directly to the edge.

Hercules's back bows and he fists the sheets. I watch Hades swallow him down and it feels like I'm on fire. This was supposed to take the edge off, but the desire is so much stronger now. It's like every time I come, every time Hercules comes, our needs becomes a hydra and multiplies.

I have to have them inside me. I can't wait.

I reach for him, but he catches my wrists. "Ah ah."

"But—"

"*This* is your punishment, love." He presses a quick kiss to my lips and I shiver at the taste of Hercules. Hades tows me to the edge of the bed and gently guides me to my feet. He looks at me and then at Hercules, who's already growing hard again, his blue eyes burning with the same desire threatening to incinerate me. "Since apparently I wasn't clear enough previously, let me elaborate. No fucking. No cocks, no hands, no mouths, no toys."

"And if we disobey?"

He gives Hercules a long look. "If you disobey, we'll reschedule the public scene tonight."

"*What?*"

His lips curve the tiniest bit. "One day you'll learn that punishments weren't created to be enjoyed, little Hercules." He walks into the bathroom and I hear the sink running. A few minutes later, Hades emerges to find us exactly where he left us. He gives that little smile again. "I'll see you in a few hours."

I sink onto the edge of the mattress the moment the door shuts. "That backfired spectacularly."

"It always does." Hercules laughs and rolls off the bed. Thwarted desire doesn't seem to bother him much, but then he rolls with the punches better than anyone else I know. He kisses me and moves away before I can sink into it. "Let's take a shower and get ready."

"I can't promise I'll keep my hands to myself."

He gives me an arch look over his shoulder. "I guess I'll have to maintain control for both of us, because there's no way in hell we're rescheduling tonight. We both know Hades doesn't bluff."

The reminder dims my temptation to test our sanctions. Hercules is right. If we keep toeing the line, Hades will slap us down. We'll deserve it, too. Sometimes the pleasure is worth the punishment, but this one won't be, especially since Hades ensured we took the edge off.

I sigh. "Being responsible is no fun."

"Aw, Meg." Hercules takes my hand and pulls me after him into the bathroom. "Don't be too sad. You get to peg my ass tonight."

"You're impossible." I laugh. "But you're right. Planning all the delicious things I'm going to do to you is enough to cheer me right up." I slap his ass and move past him into the shower. "Love you."

"Love you, too, Meg." He sounds kind of in awe of it, like it just hit him that this is our life and it's real. *We're* real.

We're happy. Really, really happy.

～

THIS SHORT ORIGINALLY APPEARED AS the November 2019 short for my Patreon. Each month, patrons nominate their favorite couples and characters, vote on one, and I write a brand new short featuring the winner. For more bonus stories, please consider joining my Patreon.

5

GOING PUBLIC, PART 2

HERCULES

Hercules

I've been in the public playroom dozens of times since I moved into the Underworld, all without actually *playing*. It feels different tonight, and it's not just because it's filled to the brim with powerful people. Each set of couches are filled, and as I follow Hades and Meg on their winding journey to the middle of the room, I belatedly realize that there are exactly the same number of groupings as there are territories in Carver City.

Every territory leader is here tonight.

"Eyes forward, little Hercules." Hades doesn't look over his shoulder to ensure I hear his murmur. He simply assumes I'll hear and obey because any other option is unthinkable. He's right.

I focus on the middle of his back. He's wearing one of his customary black on black suits, and looks particularly dapper tonight. This scene might be for us, but it's also for show, too. Appearances matter. I shift my attention to Meg, which is a mistake because she's distracting as hell. She's wearing trousers and a cropped bustier thing that leaves a large swathe of her stomach bare and puts her breasts on display.

A space in the center of the room is cleared except for a St. Andrew's cross and a chest that isn't identical to the one in our bedroom, but is close enough that I have no doubts about what it contains. My body goes hot and I have to concentrate to muscle down my physical reaction.

Hades flicks his fingers, and I obey instantly, folding into a kneeling position in the center of the space. I swear I can actually *feel* the attention of everyone in the room as their gazes trace my bare chest and back, examine the tiny black shorts Meg picked out earlier, flick over my thighs and feet. I keep my gaze on the floor in front of me. I'm not running this show, and the relief is enough to make me shake. I trust Hades and Meg to take me where I need to, but I didn't expect to be so overwhelmed by the audience.

I catch sight of Meg's trousers a moment before her fingers feather through my hair. "Breathe, Hercules. Just breathe. He's got us." She speaks low, the words for me and me alone.

I obey. I was never going to do anything but obey.

I half expect Hades to give some kind of speech, but I should know better by now. Everyone is aware of why we're here, and Hades isn't one to waste time grandstanding when his actions can speak for him.

"On the cross, little Hercules." He doesn't raise his voice, but I hear every word all the same.

I'm already moving to obey before my mind fully registers the command. There was a time when I'd question that, but we're long past it. I position myself in front of the St. Andrew's cross. Meg's hands are the ones that begin to fasten me to it, cuffing my wrists up at the top of each section of the X. She double-checks the tightness and then trails her fingers down my arms, nails lightly scratching.

I shiver and bite my bottom lip. It's nothing close to pain, but the promise of things to come chases away a bit of my nervousness.

Hades walking around to stand before me chases away the rest. There's a wealth of warmth in his eyes, and it's just for us. No one else in the room matters. "Do you remember the first scene we did together?"

"Of course." It was Meg on the cross that time, and it felt like the moment when we all crossed the point of no return with each other. I didn't recognize it at the time, but then I was still wrapped up in twelve different kinds of confusion when it came to these two. I'm not now.

I'm where I'm supposed to be.

More, I'm *happy* to be here.

"This is a new beginning of sorts." He speaks softly, just for me. "There's no going back from this."

I manage a smile. "There was no going back from it the moment I fell for both of you."

"True enough." He shifts to the side, looking to where I can hear Meg digging through the chest. "Your safe word."

"Olympus."

"You may begin."

I have half a second of thinking he's talking to me before I feel the first bite of the flogger against my back. It stings more than hurts, but I gasp all the same. Hades watches my face, the heat in his eyes rising with each strike. He leans in and presses a soft kiss to my lips, and then he's gone, disappearing behind me.

I close my eyes. I don't think I mind being on display, but I want to preserve the intimacy of this moment, pretend it's just us in this big room. Without my sight, I have a better awareness of what's going on behind me. Hades's footsteps moving to where Meg stands. The soft sound of his hand stroking over some part of her body. Her little inhale.

And then she picks up her pace and I know nothing but heat and the delicious curl of pain that promises pleasure to come. Not yet, though. First, they'll work me into a frenzy of need.

I'm already there.

My hips move almost on their own, grinding against the padded section of the cross, the pressure good but nowhere near good enough. My breath shudders out with each exhale, need coloring every sound I make.

"Think he's had enough, love?"

Meg's laugh is a little mean, and I nearly moan aloud at the sound. "He'll take as much as we want to give."

"I have something special I want to *give*."

"By all means."

More movement, more rustling through the chest. I'm focused so hard on listening, I startle at the feeling of Hades's hands stroking over my back. It hurts and feels good, all at the same time. I can't hold back my moan any longer, especially when he dips his fingers into the waist-band of my shorts and tugs them down the barest fraction of an inch.

Then Hades is there, pressing his entire body against mine. The soft friction of his suit against my back draws another moan from my lips. "*Fuck*."

"You can take more."

It's not in the realm of a question, but I answer it all the same. "I can take more."

He brushes his lips against the back of my neck and snakes his hand around to grip my cock through my shorts. "So eager." He strokes me a few times, until I'm fighting not to grind against his hand. I shake from fighting that urge, but I know all too well if I move, he'll stop this delicious torture. I don't want him to stop. Not yet. Not ever.

And then Meg's there as well, her smaller hands joining Hades as he idly strokes my cock. She dips down and cups my balls and makes a happy noise. "Are you ready for me to take your ass, Hercules?"

I think I might die if she doesn't. "Yes," I gasp.

She pulls my shorts halfway down my thighs. Hades's hand immediately returns to my cock, stroking me enough to keep me on the edge, but not quite enough to send me over.

Then Meg bites my ass.

I curse and jerk forward, and Hades laughs. "So mean."

"Can you blame me?" She squeezes me and presses a kiss to where I just felt her teeth. "He's got such a pert little ass. It was begging for my teeth."

"It's begging for something else now."

"I'd be a shame if we left him hanging."

They're standing here touching me, talking about me as if I'm not present. I hate it. I love it. I bite my bottom lip to keep silent, even as I want to beg them to stop teasing me and finish this. I feel like I've been riding the edge for weeks, instead of the few hours since Hades told us we weren't allowed to fuck.

One of them spreads cool lube over me and then the hard head of Meg's strap-on is pressing into me. I tense and then relax into it. I don't have control right now. I don't have to do anything but submit. There's a delirious freedom in that. I let my head hang forward, let them keep fucking me with hand and dildo even as my chest aches from each breath. I'm shaking and fighting to hold still and it's so hot, I can barely stand it.

And then Meg is seated entirely within me, her narrow hips against my ass. She reaches around and strokes over my chest, as if her breasts against my back aren't causing the most heavenly agony. "You're doing wonderfully."

I exhale a shaky sigh that turns into a moan when she pinches my nipples. "If Hades doesn't stop playing with my cock, I'm going to come."

Hades's dark chuckle is his only response. He doesn't stop stroking me, doesn't change the pace or pressure in the least. "You'll come when we allow it."

"Not yet," Meg says.

Then she starts fucking me.

It feels... I don't have words for how good it feels to have her taking my ass while Hades strokes my cock. I feel owned and possessed and undeniably *theirs*.

"Open your eyes, little Hercules." Hades's voice is soft in my ear. "Look at the way they lust after what's ours."

I obey. I'm helpless to do anything else.

The cross and my position keep me from seeing all but a small sliver of the room, but I see a gathering of couches filled with people watching me with hungry eyes. Watching *us*. My breath catches in my chest, the pleasure nearly unbearable. "I'm close," I grind out. When Hades doesn't respond, doesn't stop, panic flickers through me. "Can I come?"

Hades leans close as Meg thrusts into me. His lips brush my ear "Yes."

Just like that, my orgasm hits me hard enough to buckle my knees. I come in great spurts, moaning and fucking Hades's hand as much as I'm able to, each thrust shoving me back onto Meg's strap-on. And then my legs give out entirely and it's only the cuffs around my wrists that keep me upright.

Hades steps closer yet and Meg eases out of me. I'm vaguely aware of her moving at my back and him working to undo the cuffs, and then they're pressed to either side of me, guiding me to the empty couch situated near our scene.

A blanket appears from somewhere and Hades wraps it around me. Meg cuddles up to me from one side and kisses me. "You did so good."

"I'm pleased," Hades says from the other side. He guides me to lean against his side and sifts his fingers through my hair. "You did well."

I still can't quite catch my breath. We've done more intense things together, but somehow this feels different. Maybe because of the audience. Maybe because it's a public declaration of *us*. I inhale slowly. "I love you."

"I know."

"Hades," Meg hisses, but there's laughter in her voice. "Try again."

His lips quirk. "I love you, too." His gaze flicks from me to Meg and back again. "Both of you."

"Good." Meg makes a happy noise and snuggles closer. "Now let Hercules catch his breath and then we can continue this In private."

Hades chuckles. "Insatiable."

"Stop pretending like that's not a good thing."

"I wouldn't dream of it being anything else." He catches her hand and brings her hand up to kiss her knuckles. But when he speaks, it's for me. "Rest, little Hercules. You have a long night ahead of you."

I let myself relax against him, his racing heart against my ear. "I can't wait."

6

TINK'S PUNISHMENT

TINK

Maybe one day it won't feel strange to be back in the Underworld as a territory leader, but I'm not there yet. I have a feeling I won't be there for a long time. Still, it's weirdly nice to spend time in a place that holds so many good memories for me. Three of the sources of those memories are seated around the booth we camped out in hours ago. It's almost time for Allecto and Aurora's shifts to start, and Meg will no doubt be occupied as well once that happens, but we're milking our time together down to the last second.

I sip my fruity drink. "You know, it's totally okay if we meet somewhere that isn't the Underworld."

"Next time." Meg's lounging in the middle of the booth's curve, a place where she can see the entirety of the lounge. "But you know the old saying about the mice playing while the cat's away; with all three of us gone, people are bound to get up to no good."

That's why we're here tonight. We're celebrating Aurora's promotion into my vacated position as Meg's second-in-command. I lift my glass. "I've said it before, but I'm feeling sentimental enough to say it about half a dozen more times. Congrats, Aurora. You're going to rock this." She'll bring a totally different take to the position than I did, but I think it will be to everyone's benefit. I grin. "Just try not to set anyone on fire in the meantime."

"*Tink*." Her light brown skin turns dusky. "I'm never going to live that down, am I?"

"No way. That was badass as hell. Tell her, Allecto."

Allecto's grin is knife-sharp. "If you ever get tired of playing with these assholes, I'd take you on my security team in a heartbeat."

"Stop poaching my people." Meg narrows her eyes, but she's smiling. "Though if you want to do some training with Allecto, you're more than welcome."

"Yeah, I'll allow it."

"Really?" Aurora's dark eyes go wide. "You don't let anyone train with your team."

"Not just anyone threatens to *burn this motherfucker to the ground* in defense of a friend." Allecto toasts Aurora with her water. "I'd say you've earned the privilege."

Aurora covers her face with her hands, but I can see her smile peeking out. "I would like that a lot."

"Monday at seven." Allecto turns that sharp smile in my direction. "Apparently we've kept you too long, Tink. Your man has come to collect you."

Meg and Aurora make playfully mocking *oooooh* sounds and I roll my eyes, even as a blush works its way across my cheeks. Hook pauses in the doorway and his gaze lands on us almost immediately. He's dressed in different clothing than he was this morning, a pair of jeans and a T-shirt. I've never seen him so casual in the Underworld, and for some reason it makes my heartbeat kick up a notch.

Meg props her elbows on the table and gives him a long

look as he stops in front of our booth. "No need to hunt down your wife. We were going to return her shortly."

His grin is just as cocky as ever and he rakes a gaze over me. I'm wearing a knee-length flouncy skirt and a tank top with lace cutouts that makes my breasts look amazing. I fully intended to track him down when I got home and tempt him into taking me against the nearest horizontal surface, but this will work, too. I tilt my head to the side. "I've been gone a couple hours. Surely that doesn't require a personal retrieval."

"I missed you." He says it simply, as if this kind of statement doesn't still rock me right down to my foundations.

I make a show of looking at my phone. "I said I'd be home at eight. It's seven-thirty."

Hook shrugs, completely unrepentant. He holds out an imperial hand. "Say goodbye, Tink. It's time to go."

I raise my eyebrows, the first tingling of a challenge coursing beneath my skin. "Yeah, I don't think so. Go away and come back in thirty minutes. Then we'll leave." I can feel my friends watching with avid interest, and they're not the only ones. We're putting on a show, after all.

"Tink." He says my name slowly, the faintest hint of warning. "Do you remember what I said I'd do if you challenged me like this?"

Yes, yes, I do. Desire pulses between my thighs, but I keep my expression bored and a little belligerent. "No. Do you know what *I'll* do to *you* for making a pest of yourself?"

His grin widens. "Have it your way, beautiful girl." Hook glances at my three friends. "Excuse me, ladies."

I barely have a second to process that and then he's kneeling. He grabs my knees and jerks me to the edge of the bench. "Wait—" It's too late.

He flips up my skirt and pauses. "No panties, beautiful

girl?" Hook's eyes twinkle up at me. "Looks to me like someone was planning on being bad."

"You have no idea."

"Thought so." He wedges his hands under my ass and lifts me as he bends down to lick my pussy.

My face is so hot right now, it might as well be the surface of the sun. I can feel my friends watching, and maybe that should shame me, but it only makes it hotter. Just like when I look around the lounge and catch Gaeton leaning against the bar, grinning like a fool. "Oh fuck."

"Later," Hook murmurs against my clit.

I half expect him to torment me with teasing, but he's relentless in pursuit of my pleasure. He's intent on my orgasm, and it's like he has a timer in his head. I give up fighting it and let the wicked stroke of his tongue and the feeling of so many people watching drive me higher and higher. It's so good and so wrong, and it doesn't matter that nearly everyone in this room has seen me in varying stages of undress and orgasm. Having Hook lick my pussy to punish me is so hot, I can barely stand it.

I dig my fingers into his hair and try to hold out, but he knows my body too well. Seconds later, I'm coming, clamping my lips together to keep from crying out.

A slow clap starts behind me and is quickly picked up around the room. I reluctantly open my eyes to find every single person applauding. Hook flips my skirt down and rises to press a quick kiss to my lips. "Come home with me now and I'll let you ride my cock in the car."

"Better go or he'll fuck you on the table," Aurora stage-whispers. "On second thought, maybe stay and keep the show going."

I can barely work up a fake glare in her direction. "You are all assholes."

"Yep," Allecto says. "And you love it."

Meg shakes her head, a small smile on her lips. "Same time next month?"

"I wouldn't miss it."

Hook catches my hand and pulls me to my feet. This time I don't resist. I give my friends a wave and let my husband tow me out of the lounge, past all the people still clapping like assholes. I manage to blow a snarky kiss to Gaeton and then we're through the door.

I barely wait until we're in the elevator to push Hook against the wall and kiss him. I can taste myself on his lips and it makes me crazy. "I don't know if I can wait to get to the car."

He turns us until my back hits the elevator wall and reaches around to push the *stop* button. I lean back to raise my eyebrows. "Hades isn't going to like that."

"He'll get over it. My wife needs my cock and she can't wait." Hook dips down and catches the backs of my thighs, lifting and spreading me. "My pants."

I waste no time unbuttoning his jeans and dragging his zipper down. I'm in no more mood to tease him now than he was to tease me earlier. "I need you. Now."

"Security people are watching." He lifts me a little higher and then his cock is there, easing into me. "You know how they like to gossip. By tomorrow everyone will know how needy you are for my cock, beautiful girl."

I'm trying to breathe past the fullness that is him. I dig my fingers into his hair and tug his mouth up to mine. "Just like everyone in the lounge knows how needy you are to get your mouth all over my pussy."

"Fuck yes I am." He thrusts, picking up a relentless rhythm. "My favorite kind of punishment."

I can't concentrate enough to keep talking, can only

whimper as he fucks me against the wall. Each stroke rubs his cock against that sweet spot inside me and his pelvis drags against my clit and, *fuck*, it's so good I can barely stand it. "Keep doing that. Make me come again."

"Greedy girl." But he obeys, adjusting his angle so that he's exactly where I need him. Again and again and again, until pressure spills over into pleasure and I can't stop myself from coming all over his cock. I force my eyes open so I see the exact moment his own pleasure takes hold. He thrusts hard into me and growls my name as he orgasms.

A tinny voice sounds from the speaker next to the elevator buttons. "If you're quite finished, release the elevator. We have guests waiting."

Hook meets my gaze and we both burst into laughter. It feels just as good as the orgasms, a lightness settling in my chest that never seems to go away these days. He lets me off the wall and we take a few seconds to adjust our clothing. Every time our eyes catch, we dissolve into giggles again. Hook hits the button to get the elevator moving and I'm blushing like a teenager when we reach the garage and the doors open to reveal Malone and Ursa. Seeing these two together isn't that odd—they're friends, best I can tell—but they both give us long looks.

Malone shakes her head. "Newlyweds."

"Cute and sickening, all at the same time." Ursa steps back so we can move out of the way. "Belated congrats on your nuptials."

"Thanks." Hook manages to hold it together until we're safely back in his SUV and pulling out of the garage. He tugs me as close as seatbelts will allow and presses a kiss to my temple.

I take his hand and lift it to run his knuckles along my

cheek. "Is it weird that acting like a pair of horny teenagers makes me deliriously happy?"

"No. Not weird at all." He looks more content than I've ever seen him, totally relaxed and at ease. "Neither of us had what you'd call normal teenage years. Might be fun to reclaim some of those experiences." Hook shoots me a look. "Want to dress up like a cheerleader and let me seduce you under the bleachers?"

"Hell yes." I'm already nodding. "But only if you wear a leather jacket and play the ultimate bad boy."

Hook chuckles. "Someone's harboring more fantasies." He coasts his hand up my bare thigh. Not exactly to seduce; more like he just enjoys touching me as much as I enjoy being touched by him. "Whatever you want, beautiful girl. We have our whole lives to play out each and every fantasy in that sexy brain of yours."

I lean up and brush my lips across his. "Let's start tonight. I want you to tie me up again."

He goes still. "You sure?"

I've never been more sure of anything. I don't have to hide anymore. I love this man, and I want everything he has to give and more. "One hundred percent." I smile. "I love you, husband."

An expression of wonderment flickers over his face, as if he can't quite believe we're in this happy place any more than I can. "I love you too, wife."

7

ROUGH DAY

TINK

I barely look up at the bedroom door opens. It's been a long day, but it's not over yet, and I can't afford to get distracted before I reach a good stopping point on this dress. "Give me thirty minutes. I'm almost done with this bit."

"Don't rush."

The strange sound in Hook's voice brings my head up. I freeze, barely managing to get my foot off the sewing machine pedal in time. He's *covered* in blood. "Jameson?"

"Ah." He looks down at his hands, his expression closed down tighter than I've ever seen it. "It's not mine."

I carefully set the fabric down and rise, racking my brain for an explanation. Since Peter died, things have been smooth-enough sailing. I'm not naive enough to believe it will continue like that indefinitely, not when we live in the world we do, but I'd hoped for more than a few months. Apparently I *am* a bit naive despite my best efforts.

Hook looks at me and I don't like how empty his dark eyes are. I don't like that he's closing himself off from me. I won't allow it.

I cross to him and stop just short of touching him. The temptation rises to demand an explanation, to push him to let me in, but I change course at last moment. Hook will tell me when he's ready. I have to believe that.

So I jerk my chin toward the bathroom. "Let's get you cleaned up."

"You don't have to." He still doesn't sound like himself.

"I know." I walk into the bathroom, holding my breath until I hear him following. It takes a few seconds to get the shower going and then I return to find him reaching for the buttons of his shirt with hands that shake. "Let me."

"Tink."

"Let me," I repeat.

He finally drops his hands and I waste no time working the buttons free. His shirt is tacky with blood and it clings to his skin as I peel it off his body. He shudders out a breath. "You're not going to ask me what happened?"

"You'll tell me when you're ready." I finish wrestling his shirt off his arms and reach for his pants.

"I can handle this bit." He gets his pants off quickly enough and tosses them on top of the shirt. Hook hesitates, something almost vulnerable crossing his face. "Join me?"

Any other time, I'd tell him to shower by himself because I have work to finish, but this isn't any other time. He needs me right now, and the work can wait a bit longer. "Sure." I strip quickly and follow him into the shower.

Hook heads directly into the water and ducks his head under the spray. I hang back and watch the water run red. Even without his clothes, there's so much blood. I doubt the person it belongs to is still among the living.

The thought should probably bother me. A normal woman would have questions and demands for answers if her husband came home like this. She might be packing her bags right now and calling the cops.

The only thing I can think of is how hurt he looks. He wouldn't take a life unless there was no other recourse left to him. I might doubt many things in my life, but I will never doubt that. I will never doubt *him*.

He scrubs his skin, over and over again, and the aching in my heart gets more intense. "Let me do your back."

It's only when he turns from me that he speaks. "It was a challenge in a roundabout way. Trip went after Nigel's girlfriend."

I stop scrubbing his back. "Is Laura okay?"

"Yes. She held him off and made enough of a racket that Nigel got there before Trip did more than split her lip." His shoulders shift under my hands. "I handled the rest."

I slip my arms around him and hug his back. It's only this close that I realize little shakes are working through his body. "You did what you had to do."

"I know." He takes a big breath and an even longer exhale. "I'm fine."

"It's okay if you're not."

Hook shifts and turns in my arms. I look up to find the tiniest bit of mirth in his dark eyes. "I half expected you to kick my ass over this."

That stings a little, but I push the emotional reaction away. Even after months together, we're still figuring each other out. We each have our histories and old wounds, and that means sometimes we unintentionally prod at them in each other. Sometimes it's intentional because we're both a little bit of an asshole.

I cup his face, his beard tickling my palms. "Being the head of the territory means sometimes you have to do fucked up shit. I can admit that I don't like it while still understanding that days like today are what keep us safe the rest of the time." I shift my hands to the back of his neck. "You made an example of him."

It's not a question, but he answers it all the same. "I did."

"Then the next person who comes after one of ours might hesitate." I tug him down until his forehead is pressed against mine. "I am sorry you have to bear the burden of it."

"It's what I signed up for."

Yes, it is. But not because he wanted the power. Because he had no other option, not if he wanted to keep the people he cared about safe. "That doesn't mean it doesn't hurt you."

His exhale ghosts across my lips. "No. It doesn't mean it doesn't hurt." Hook strokes his hands down my body to rest on my hips. "I need..."

I'm already nodding. "Yes."

He lifts his head enough to smirk at me, though it's still a ghostly impression of his usual arrogance. "You didn't even wait for me to finish that sentence."

"I don't have to." I step closer, pressing myself to his body. "You need. It's that simple. I'm saying yes. Also that simple."

Hook shakes his head slowly. "Just when I think I can't love you more."

"It's a mutual affliction." I smile. "Tell me what you need."

"I just need you, Tink." He backs toward the shower bench, towing me with him. I expect him to sit on it, but he guides me to bend down and brace my hands on it instead. "It's going to be fast and rough."

Need courses through me. "Do your worst."

He kicks my legs wider and palms me between my thighs, fingers pushing into me slowly. Even in this, even when need is riding him hard, he ensures I'm ready for him. And then Hook's cock is there, replacing his fingers. He grips my hips as he fucks me, and for once he's chasing his own pleasure. I don't mind. I can't take away the pain he's experiencing, but I can give him this. I *want* to give him this.

Hook drives into me again and again, his fingers tightening as he pulls me back to meet each thrust. It's rough and brutal and I'm fighting to keep my arms braced because it feels so damn good. Every stroke hits a spot deep inside me that has my toes curling against the tiled floor. He growls my name as he comes, grinding his hips against my ass, pushing himself deeper yet.

Only then does his touch go soft on me, his hands smoothing over my hips and ass and up my back to pull me to my feet. Hook turns me and then his mouth is on mine. The kiss is the exact opposite of what we just did, sweet and devastatingly gentle. I don't know if it's an apology or a thank you, but it doesn't matter because when he lifts his head, he looks more like himself.

Hook smooths my hair back from my face. "Thank you."

"I enjoyed it." I tow him down for a quick kiss. "Want to hang out while I finish Isabelle's wedding dress?"

His brows wing up. "Already? You only started it a few days ago."

"I'm inspired." And it makes me happy to see two people I care about find their happiness with her. I wasn't sure they'd pull it off, but apparently they have, and this is my little contribution to their happily ever after.

Hook reaches around me to turn off the water. "Sorry for interrupting."

"Don't be." I stretch my arms over my head and something pops in my back. "I needed the break, and you needed me. It all works out."

His low grin has my stomach doing a happy flip. "How about I make the quick sex up to you when you're done?"

"I'm listening."

"A massage." He catches my hand and lifts it to his lips, his eyes dancing. "A handful of orgasms. Cuddling afterward."

He'll be okay. I understood that, of course, but I can actually see him settling back into his skin, back into the person he is. Hook will always doubt himself after he's forced to do something like this. It makes me love him more that it affects him. He might be a villain to many, but he's mine.

I grin. "You have yourself a deal."

"Good." He waits until I step past him to swat my ass. "Get to work. I'll work us up some dinner in the meantime."

I glance at him over my shoulder. "I love you."

His smile is almost free of the shadows that plagued him when he first arrived back in our rooms. "I love you, too. Always."

"Always," I repeat, my happiness bubbling up in my chest like a live thing. Some days I can barely believe that this is my life. Even with the darkness, it's better than I could have dreamed. I wouldn't trade it for anything.

THIS SHORT ORIGINALLY APPEARED AS the April 2020 short for my Patreon. Each month, patrons nominate their favorite couples and characters, vote on one, and I write a brand new short featuring the winner. For more bonus stories, please consider joining my Patreon.

8

THE BABY TALK
TINK

"Do you want to talk about it?"

I jump, and then instantly feel silly for jumping. I've been sitting on the couch long enough for the sun to change position in the sky, dropping down to kiss the horizon. I *should* have been working, but I'm too distracted and I can't trust myself to cut fabric right now. I pull the blanket I've draped over my shoulders more firmly around me. "Talk about what?"

"Uh huh." Hook drops down next to me and stretches out. He's wearing a suit, but he's removed both shoes and socks, which means he's been home for more than a few minutes.

I didn't even notice. I shiver. "How was your day?"

"Fine. Gloriously mundane. But we're not talking about me. We're talking about why you're sitting here, impersonating a human burrito." He glances at his watch. "Normally, I have to tear you away from work and bribe you with orgasms and food. Are you not feeling well?"

I'm not, but not in the way he means. "I'm not sick."

Hook sits up, his brows drawing together. "Okay, now I'm actually worried. What's going on?"

It's so tempting, even after all this time, to shut him out and roll around in my misery alone. It's all in my head. I know that. I *know* that. It changes nothing. But Hook is tenacious and, really, I don't *really* want to suffer alone.

I take a shaking breath. "What if I'm a terrible mother?"

He blinks. The shock on his face might have made me laugh if I wasn't so in my head right now. He grabs my legs and tows them up and over his lap, turning me to face him fully. The trademark grin is nowhere in sight, leaving him devastatingly serious. "Why would you think that?"

"We know we want kids, right?" I want a family. I've always wanted a family. But that doesn't mean I should have one. Some people shouldn't procreate. How am I supposed to tell if I'm one of them? The thought makes my chest hurt. "I haven't exactly had any good parental role models. My foster parents weren't terrible, but they were overworked and exhausted all the time, and I was just another mouth to feed. A burden."

"Tink—"

"I know how this sounds, but please let me get it out."

His dark eyes are just as warm as the blanket around my shoulders. "You've been sitting here, thinking about this all afternoon, haven't you?"

"Yes." Longer, if I'm honest, but today the thoughts have gone from flitting through my head to feeling like they're a bus trying to mow me over.

He rubs his hands lightly over my legs. "I'm listening."

"What if we have kids and I fuck them up? I'm mean, Hook. I don't know how to temper my tone or filter my words. I've never bothered to learn how. If we have kids, they're going to have a mean asshole of a mother and they're going to end up needing a lifetime of therapy as a result." My breath catches in my throat, and I clamp my lips together, determined to keep the rest of the poisoned words in.

"Tell me," he says quietly. He takes my hand, linking our fingers, and squeezes. "Tell me the rest, Tink."

I don't want to. I really, really don't want to. I close my eyes and exhale. "What if I turn into my mother? She just dropped me as a baby at a fucking fire station. What if I go all the way through the pregnancy and then have buyer's remorse and just bounce? Aren't you worried about that?"

"No."

I open my eyes. "What?"

Hook holds my gaze. "Are you worried that someday I'm going to hit you? Or hit our theoretical kids? Just get mad enough that I lose all control and do it?"

I flinch, anger rushing up and eclipsing my misery. "No. Fuck no. You'd never do that."

"My father did." His smile is bitter.

I open my mouth to snarl at him, and then force myself to slow down and think about what he's saying. He's right. Of course he's right. "I see your point, but it doesn't make the fear less real."

"I know." He tugs on my hands until I let him move me onto his lap so he can wrap his arms around me. He's better than any blanket, and I relax back against him, letting his strength bolster me. Hook kisses my temple. "Neither of us have great childhoods to pull from. It doesn't matter. We're not our parents and we're more than the trauma we've experienced." He cuddles me closer. "You're going to be a great mom, Tink. Fierce and protective and someone who shows her kids what strength and ambition looks like. And love. So much love."

I lay my head against his shoulder. It feels like he's lifted a hundred pounds of fear from my shoulders. "How do you always know the right thing to say?"

"Not always." Hook chuckles. "But, to tell you the truth, I've been thinking about it, too."

"Thinking about it..."

"Thinking about taking our talk of kids into a reality." He must feel me tense, because he rubs one hand down my back in a soothing stroke. "Not until you're ready."

"What if I'm never ready?" I don't know why I ask the question. We've come so far beyond my needing to test him with theoretical questions. But I'm feeling weak and scared right now, and I need Hook's words to build back up my foundations.

He hugs me tighter. "Then you're never ready, and we don't have kids. And we'll still be happy and fulfilled and live out our happily ever after."

I don't know why I can't stop poking at this. I already know what I want. I already know that Hook loves me enough that this won't break us, no matter where I land on the subject of kids. But the nearly overwhelming desire to keep questioning is there, pressing against the inside of my lips.

Won't you resent me if we don't have kids?

Won't you stop trusting me?

Won't...

I lean back and look up at him. There was a time when I'd fight in order to avoid being vulnerable, but we've long since passed it. I bite my bottom lip, hating that my throat feels thick. "Once we make that call, there's no changing our mind or hitting the reset. You can't have buyer's remorse on a baby."

He smooths my hair back, his expression achingly

gentle. "There's nothing saying we need to do it now. We can wait."

For once, he's not getting it. I wrap my hands around his wrists. "That's just it. I don't want to wait. I want babies, Hook. Multiple babies. I want them so bad, it scares the shit out of me. Which is why I'm sitting here, freaking myself out with all the things that can go wrong."

He's gone so still, I'm not sure he's breathing. "What are you saying?"

After everything I've just dumped on him, it makes no sense that *this* is what trips me up. I gather up every scrap of courage I have. "I want... Do you want to have a baby? With me? Like in, say, nine months or so?" He's still staring at me, so I start babbling. "My annual appointment is next week, and it'd be really easy to get the IUD taken out. I think we have to wait a month after that before we can really start trying, but that just gives us plenty of time to practice..." I trail off. Hook's eyes are shining a little. Oh fuck, did I mess this up, too? I tighten my grip on his wrists. "I don't have to, though. We can wait. I can make an appointment to take it out whenever. Or never. Because if you're not ready—"

"Tink." His voice is hoarse. "Beautiful girl, I'm ready."

My breath catches in my throat. "Really?"

"Yes." He breaks into a heart-stopping grin. "If you are, yes, a thousand times fucking yes." Hook makes a valiant effort to temper his excitement. "But if you change your mind, that's more than okay, too."

My chest feels both tight and achingly light at the same time. I find myself grinning right back. "Really? You really mean it?"

"Fuck yes." He cups my face and presses a light kiss to my lips. "Our kids are going to be hellions. You know that, right? They'll be climbing the walls and spitting attitude and driving us crazy."

"I know," I whisper. "I can't wait."

It doesn't seem possible, but he grins harder, beaming at me. "I love you."

"I love you, too." I wiggle out of the blanket and shift to straddle him. "Think Allecto will agree to babysit?"

For a second, actual alarm flickers through his joy. "You're joking, right? She'll have the kid for an hour and be teaching them knife-work."

"Mmm." I drape my arms around his neck. There's still a tiny bit of unease, but I don't know if I'll ever truly banish it. From what I understand, most parents live in fear of fucking up their kids. I guess that makes me startlingly *normal*, at least in this. I don't know why that's weirdly reassuring, but it is. Regardless, it feels like talking through it was enough to take away the worst of the fear, paving the way for excitement to take hold. "Want to start practicing now?"

He hooks an arm around my waist and turns, bearing me down to the couch. "Fuck yeah." Hook settles between my thighs. But instead of kissing me, he props himself on his elbows and looks down at me. "Thank you for telling me what you were feeling. I know that shit doesn't come easy to you, and I value the trust you put in me."

Gods, he's going to make my heart melt with that kind of talk. I reach up and cup his jaw, his beard tickling my palm. "It's not easy, no, but you make it easier. I know I'm a mess; I'm going to be a mess for our entire lives."

He turns his head and kisses my palm. "Haven't you figured it out by now, wife? We're both messes. That's the human condition. It doesn't define us any more than any one thing does. It's just part of us."

"When did you get so smart?"

He pretends to think. "Well, I married this really smart lady. She's kind of an asshole sometimes, but she makes me up my game."

That startles a laugh out of me. "I'm not the only one who's an asshole."

"Guilty."

"And you're right. Our kids are probably going to be assholes, too."

He grins. "Good thing I'm great at dealing with assholes then, huh?"

I give his shoulders a playful shove, toppling him off the couch and onto the floor. I don't expect him to take me with him, but I land on my knees, straddling his waist. I frown down at him. "Was this all a ploy to get me to ride your cock?"

"Nah." He pushes up my skirt, his fingers unerringly finding my panties. "It's so you can sit on my face."

That startles a laugh out of me. "Well, when you put it like that, how can I resist?"

"You can't." He shifts down until his head is between my thighs and presses a kiss to my pussy through my panties. "Just close your eyes and try to enjoy it."

"Mmm." I whimper as he keeps kissing me.

Hook always knows what I need. Whether it's tough conversations or orgasms or cuddles. The last of my doubts drift away against the onslaught of pleasure he deals. He's right. We'll probably stumble and fuck up, but we aren't our parents. Our children will be loved and taken care of and fucking *happy.*

This is our happily ever after.

～

THIS SHORT ORIGINALLY APPEARED AS the September 2020 short for my Patreon. Each month, patrons nominate their favorite couples and characters, vote on one, and I write a brand new short featuring the winner. For more bonus stories, please consider joining my Patreon.

9

VALENTINE'S DAY IN THE UNDERWORLD

AURORA

February 2019 Patreon
Valentine's Day in the Underworld
Aurora

EVERYTHING IS as it should be.

The club won't open for another ten minutes, but I'm finally starting to understand why Meg and Tink used to make the rounds through the empty rooms before each shift. There's a strange kind of ownership one feels when they know that *they're* responsible.

I wasn't sure about taking the promotion when Meg offered. I am not Tink. I'll never be Tink. She's so fierce and unafraid and willing to step to any line drawn in the sand to ensure those under her are protected. I'm not fierce. I don't remember what it's like to be unafraid, though I have long since learned to hide my fear. Once, my survival depended on it. Now, it's both habit and a comfort. Even my friends only see what I let them see. It's better that way. Simpler.

How am I supposed to explain the truth?

Hades saved me, though he'll never admit as much. The one time I pressed him, he claimed it was a deal like any other, but he conveniently forgets to mention that I had nothing to offer. Just myself, broken as I am. It shouldn't be enough for someone like Hades, not in exchange for all he's done for me. And yet here we are, years later and untold experience grown.

It *should* make me less afraid, less likely to wait for the other foot to drop. But the longer this strange fortune lasts, the more sure I am that when it's time to pay the piper, the cost will be higher than I can comprehend.

But that day is not today. Another twenty-four-hour cycle passed and an incoming bullet I continue to dodge. I've learned to appreciate these things, learned to cling to the half full bit of the glass and embrace life with everything I have. It's not forever, after all.

"Aurora."

I turn as Meg walks into the public playroom. She's dressed in what's become her customary sexy menswear; tonight it's wide-legged trousers and a vest that displays her breasts to perfection. Her dark hair is pulled back into a sleek ponytail and her red lipstick is flawless. She gives me a warm smile. "You ready for tonight?"

"Of course." I look around the room again. "Though I'd be more ready if you and Hades weren't so adverse to Valentine's Day décor." Every table in the room has a classy vase containing a bouquet of red roses. It creates a pretty picture, but it's nowhere near the level Hercules and I wanted to bring to the place.

"It's tacky." She slings an arm around my shoulders and gives me a squeeze. "And weirdly triggering for some of the people who come here to forget about the people they're in love with and can't be with."

I know exactly who she's talking about. Gaeton and Beast. I'm sure there are others, but they're the two who have kept everyone captivated since they broke off their respective relationships with Isabelle Belmont a year ago. The fact that both are grieving the Man in Black this Valentine's Day only makes things more complicated. "I'm sure it will be fine."

"It will be." She says it with such confidence, a shiver of unease goes through me. Meg gives me another squeeze and releases me. "Now that Alaric's back in town, I have him on Beast tonight. I'd like you to take Gaeton."

My unease fades. What she's asking is easy enough. I enjoy scening with Gaeton. He can be brash and arrogant, but he's got an ooey-gooey center and he's incredibly tender during aftercare. I like Beast just fine, but I consider Gaeton a friend. "Of course. Are you sure he's going to be here tonight?"

Meg looks around the room, her dark eyes taking in every detail. "I'm sure. He'll probably be in a foul mood, too. Can you handle it?"

I try not to bristle at the question. I'm new to this position and, more, the submissive role I find easiest is the sweet virginal sub. Innocent and wide eyed and soft in every way. It's been a safe role to play, even if it's starting to chafe. "I can handle it."

"Good girl." She gifts me with another sharp smile. "Want a drink before things pick up?"

"Sure."

We end up leaning against the bar while Tisiphone pours whiskey into two glasses. I never used to have the taste for it before I came here, but Meg's brought me around. It helps that she knows what she's about and she's got expensive taste. I sip mine, reveling in the warmth that immediately spreads through my stomach. One drink isn't enough to get me anywhere near buzzed, but the warmth? The only other time I feel that sort of thing is when I'm in a scene. I crave it.

I'm facing the door, which is why I see her the moment she enters the room. Malone. She's got her white-blond hair swept back from her face and she's wearing deep green harem pants that should look absolutely ridiculous, but somehow she pulls them off. Her white blouse has a deep V, the slice of pale skin making my mouth water despite knowing better. Malone is all predator, and arguably the most dangerous person in this city, even including Hades. She's one of the few territory leaders who has a fully legit business that she's CEO of, while also ruling the less savory bits of her slice of the city with an iron fist.

She catches me watching her and holds my gaze for a long moment. I try to maintain eye contact. I do. But her dominance overwhelms me this time, just like it always has in the past, and I drop my gaze.

My next sip of whiskey isn't nearly as enjoyable as the first. It would be so easy to take it as a shot, to embrace that warmth as a distraction from the woman currently sliding into her customary booth. Instead, I slide the glass away.

"Have you considered hair of the dog?"

Meg's voice startles me, which tells me exactly how off-balance I am. I glance at her. "What?"

"You two haven't had a scene together since that first time." She watches me over the top of her glass. "Might be best to just do it again and get past whatever's going on with you."

"No." I don't mean to sound so firm, like I'm slamming the door in her face, but the thought of scening with Malone... I can't do it. I won't. I have embraced every

Dom and Domme who I've played with over the last few years, and gladly. They all have their styles and preferences, and they all respect my part in playing out our mutual fantasies.

Malone... It took her less than an hour to crack me open and break me into a thousand pieces. Maybe I could have forgiven her that, *maybe*, but she ignored me for months after that night. Continues to act like I'm an interesting piece of the background and not a person with thoughts and feelings of my own. I wasn't prepared for how much that would sting, for how much it continues to sting, and I'll be damned before I let her that close again.

Not that she's even attempted it.

I can feel my skin getting hot and angry, and I almost sag in relief when Gaeton's familiar massive form strides through the door. "Duty calls."

"Aurora."

I stop short. "Yeah?"

"You can talk to me if you need to."

I know that, but what is there to say? That Malone is the only person who tempted me into letting my heart get mixed up in things, and she's the same one who reinforced the reason I keep that part of myself locked away at all times? Meg might understand... Or she might decide to meddle. I can't take that risk, so I give her a bright smile. "I know."

I stride to Gaeton, putting a little swing in my step. Tonight I'm wearing a flirty mini skirt that swishes around my thighs and a lace bra that leaves nothing to the imagination. Thigh-high white stockings complete the pseudo schoolgirl look.

Gaeton sees me coming and gives me a grin that's a shadow of his normal one. "Hey, Aurora."

"Hey, big guy." I stop just short of touching him and give him a smile. "Want to play with me tonight?"

His smile dims, his dark eyes tormented. "I don't know if you want to deal with where my head's at tonight, honey."

If I didn't already plan on helping him forget his troubles for a little bit, his hesitance now would cement it. I take his big hand and tug him closer, wrapping him around me. Gaeton's hands can nearly bracket my waist, and the size difference sends a delightful thrill through me tonight just like it always has in the past. "Why don't you let me decide that for myself?" I hook my fingers in the band of his slacks. "I can take anything you need to give me."

He looks like he wants to argue, but finally nods. "Private room."

"Sure thing." I step back and, keeping a hold of his hand, tow him behind me through the lounge. As we pass Malone's booth, I can feel her gaze on me but I refuse to look over. It takes all of sixty seconds to make it through the mostly empty public playroom and to the halls with all the private rooms. I slow. "What would you like tonight?"

"A bed."

That's new. I steer him into one of the few rooms we keep that are set up like traditional bedrooms—with a few key additions. Once we're alone, I move to a spot right at the end of the bed and wait. "Whatever you need."

Gaeton scrubs a hand over his face. "I don't have it in me for complicated shit tonight." The look he gives me is pained and without artifice. "I need to fuck you until I can't remember my own name."

I blink, but work to shield my surprise. "Whatever you need," I repeat. I can't fix Gaeton's life, but I can give him this. I *want* to give him this.

Still he doesn't move. "Safe word."

As if he doesn't know it by heart now. I give him a faint smile. "Thorns."

"Good." He's on me before I have a chance to brace for it. He hooks his hands under my thighs and then we're on the bed, his big body pressing me against the soft mattress. Gaeton told no lies. He isn't messing around. He barely brushes a kiss to my mouth before he's moving down my body, yanking my clothes out of the way to get to the bits of me he wants. He palms my breasts and then shoves up my skirt. "No panties, Aurora." His words rumble against my pussy and then his mouth is on me.

Gaeton loves oral sex. He has for as long as I've known him. The man likes to take his time and every orgasm he coaxes from his partners seems to delight him to no end.

There's none of that tonight.

He goes after my clit as if he's angry at it, at me. We've played together enough times that he knows exactly what will get me to the edge, and he drives me there relentlessly. I might laugh if I had the breath. Trust Gaeton to need to fuck hard but make sure I come first.

He works two blunt fingers into me and presses them against my G-spot. My orgasm crashes over me like a wave I didn't see coming. I've barely reached it's crest when he's moving up my body again. A rip of a condom wrapper, the barest hesitation while he rolls it onto his cock, and then his pushing into me just as relentlessly as he's done everything else tonight. He's almost too big to make it work this fast, but my body accommodates him.

"Fuck," he breathes. "Yeah. That's what I need. Your tight little pussy clenching around my cock." But he's not looking at me. Even as he laces his fingers through mine and drives into me like the very hounds of hell are forcing him forward,

I can't shake the feeling that he's wishing I was someone else.

I don't blame him for that. He's not my person. I love him in a friendly sort of way, but Gaeton was never meant to be mine. And I was never meant to be his.

He curses and then he's coming, his strokes going harder yet, shoving me into another orgasm of my own. I wrap my legs around his waist, clinging to him in the only way I can with his hands pinning mine to the bed.

Gaeton curses and slumps to the side, pulling me with him. I barely have a chance to catch my breath before he's up and moving to dispose of the condom. I half expect him to end things there, but I shouldn't underestimate Gaeton. He flops back onto the bed next to me and gives me a worried look. "Did I hurt you?"

"Not even a little bit." I lean up on my side and give him a soft kiss. "Sometimes a rough fuck is exactly what I need, too."

He studies me, some of the pain already gone from his face. "You too sore to go again?"

This time, my smile is one hundred percent genuine. It seems kink isn't on the menu tonight. Just, as he said, fucking until he can't remember his name. "For you, big guy? I'll go as many times as you can handle."

He laughs. "Hoped you'd say that." He snags me around the waist and hauls me up his body until I'm straddling his face. "About time I worshiped this pretty pussy of yours properly." He grabs a pillow and wedges it beneath his head and gives me a grin that sends a wave of warmth through me akin to the best kind of whiskey. "Think your legs will give out before my tongue does?"

I spread my thighs a little more, lowering myself until I

can feel his breath ghosting against my clit. "Only one way to find out."

THIS SHORT ORIGINALLY APPEARED AS the February 2020 short for my Patreon. Each month, patrons nominate their favorite couples and characters, vote on one, and I write a brand new short featuring the winner. For more bonus stories, please consider joining my Patreon.

10

A BEASTLY WEDDING

ISABELLE

I didn't expect to be nervous. I pace around the small room. It didn't *feel* small when I first arrived here to wait for my cue, but now I'm sure the walls are closing in.

I shouldn't be here alone. My father should be with me, his steady presence calming the racing of my heart and offering me his assurance that this was the right choice. Maybe he'd even tell me he was proud of me for getting out of my own way.

The thought makes me smile past the tightness in my throat. I adjust my grip on the bouquet, my fingers following the two ribbons artfully hanging from the arrangement. One for my mother. One for my father. It's nowhere near a good enough replacement for the man himself, but it still feels right. I'm not sure I believe in heaven or hell, but if there's an afterlife, I hope my father is watching this moment and is pleased.

We've done it. The conflict with Ursa that threatened our borders is resolved. She'll continue to test because that's the kind of territory leader she is, but she's no longer looking to take a bite out of us.

The music changes. That's my cue.

I give myself one last shake and move to the door, careful not to step on the long flowing white masterpiece of a dress that Tink created for me. I'd argued against white, but she prevailed. I'm glad she did now. It's perfect. The off-the-shoulder style and fitted bodice hug my body and then flare gently to fall to the ground. It's a deceptively simple style, classic and expensive. I love it.

The short walk to the greenhouse feels strange and surreal. I step through the doors and pause, my breath catching in my throat. The greenhouse isn't designed for a large gathering. There are winding pathways designed to immerse a person in the beauty of the flowers and plants, all of it cumulating in a small space in the center with a few benches.

That's where I find my men.

Gaeton and Beast stand shoulder to shoulder, both of them decked out in tuxes. I have to pause again, but there's no catching my breath this time. The tuxes bring out different aspects in each of them. Gaeton looks like a barbarian king, the clothing playing up his size and ferocity. Beast looks like a fallen angel. Without normal clothes to dampen his beauty, he's so beautiful, it shorts out my brain.

Was I worried about this not being the right choice? One look at them, at the way they watch *me* walk toward them, appreciation and heat in their respective gazes. This isn't a cage. It's the first step in a new chapter for us. One I want with all my heart.

I walk up the path to them in slow steps, barely noticing the small handful of chairs filled with my sisters and Muriel on one side, and Aurora, Tink, and Hook on the other. My sisters had wanted a huge wedding like they each had, one worthy of the Belmonte name. I didn't want to share this day with anyone who I didn't care about—who my men didn't care about.

This is just for us. No one else.

Beast and Gaeton shift to the side, and David appears in the space between them. He gives me a warm smile. "You ready?"

"Yes." No hesitation. No fear. Only a heady anticipation for what comes next.

"Please take each other's hands."

We do, forming our own little triangle. Since our marriage isn't legal in the most literal sense, we ultimately decided to go with a handfasting ceremony instead. David moves around us, binding each of our forearms together with a length of red rope, speaking in a voice designed to carry to the rest of the room, talking about the commitment we're making and how it will last a year and then we'll revisit. It's all noise to me. I only have eyes for my men.

The weight of the bindings feels larger than it is. Significant. As David finishes his circle and resumes his position between Beast and Gaeton, he grins at us. "If you want to say a few words…"

Gaeton gives a rough nod. His eyes are shining and he's gripping my forearm tightly. I suspect he's doing the same to Beast's. "I promise to care for and love you both. Not just for a year. Forever."

When Beast speaks, his voice is rougher than normal. "I promise to protect and lead." He raises his brows when Gaeton snorts. "And love. You're both mine. I'm never letting you go."

Now it's my turn. The tightness in my throat is nearly overwhelming. I take an unsteady breath. "I promise to love and communicate with you both." I lean in and lower my voice. "And submit, though only in the bedroom."

The rest of the short ceremony passes in a blur. I can't focus on anything but the promise in the contact we maintain. A triangle, a triad, a throuple. Perfectly balanced in every way. We're not bound tightly but I already know I'll be feeling the weight of the ropes for a very long time.

Forever.

David carefully removes the ropes and passes them to Beast. He grins at us, happiness infusing his features. "Congratulations. You may kiss..." He waves a big hand at the three of us. "Everyone."

Beast moves first, snagging the back of Gaeton's neck and dragging him down to meet his mouth. It's a fierce kiss, barely leashed. A promise of things to come. He gives me an identical treatment, towing me to his mouth instead of coming to mine. It might make me laugh at how *Beast* it is, but I'm too busy falling into the taste of him to find any amusement in the situation. Desire sparks, and I welcome it whole-heartedly. And then his mouth is gone and I'm looking up at Gaeton. He cups my face in his hands and kisses me slowly, almost gently.

It feels like we were always on the path to this moment, to standing at the altar with the three of us. It just took several detours and a couple wrong turns to reach this destination.

The men each take one of my hands and we turn to face the room. *Both* my sisters are crying. So is Aurora. Everyone looks so incredibly happy, nearly as happy as I feel.

We walk down the aisle together, my men bracketing me in. Holding me up. Being strong so I don't have to be.

I expect us to head toward the room Cordelia had made up for our reception, but Beast picks up his pace and drags us into the little room where I'd waited earlier. I barely register Gaeton shutting the door behind me when Beast's mouth crashes down on mine. He eats my moan, swallowing the sound down even as Gaeton's hands go to the back of my dress and unlace me.

I jerk back as the dress goes slack, leaving me in only a garter and white thigh-highs. "Wait."

"Shhh." Gaeton's big hands bracket my waist and lift me up. Beast bends down and carefully takes my dress and drapes it over the small dresser. Then my feet touch down on the ground. I turn to find them kissing as they divest each other of their clothing, hands rough and unsteady.

It's so hot. Unbearably hot. I sink into the single chair in the room and skate a hand down my stomach to stroke my clit as I watch them get naked. "We're supposed to wait for tonight for this kind of thing."

Gaeton lifts his head and grins at me. "Can't wait. You two look too good."

"Up, princess." Beast grabs my hand and drags me to my feet. He pushes Gaeton into the chair to take my place. "We don't have much time."

In reality, the handful of people attending this wedding will wait as long as we need. But reality feel strange and distant while we're in this little room. *We don't have much time.* I lick my lips. "Someone could come looking for us at any minute."

"Yes." He closes his hands on my shoulders and nudges me climb onto Gaeton's lap in the chair. "You two little sluts need orgasms to get you through until tonight. Who am I to refuse you?"

I might laugh if I could draw breath. Gaeton's bracketing my hips with his hands, urging me to grind against his big cock. He grins at Beast. "It's rude to refuse your husband and wife on our wedding day."

Husband. Wife.

I shiver. This is happening. We've really done it.

They're mine and I'm theirs.

"Get on Gaeton's cock, Isabelle. Don't make me say it twice."

There will be a time when I'll play disobedient submissive and make him punish me. This afternoon isn't it. I lift myself up for Gaeton to guide his cock to my entrance. The little bit I touched myself didn't fully prepare me to be stretched wide by him, but I luxuriate in the almost-pain. It's mine, the same way they're mine. "Mine."

"Yes." Beast moves to stand next to the chair and clasps my chin. "You know what else is yours to take?" He taps my bottom lip, silently demanding I open my mouth. I obey instantly, already knowing where this is going. And then he's guiding his cock into my mouth, a long slow slide that nevertheless doesn't give me nearly enough time to adjust. He bumps the back of my throat, and I can't muscle past my gag reflex.

Beast's dark chuckle makes my whole body go tight. "Six months of fucking us, and she still needs to be taught to properly deep-throat." He pulls his cock from my mouth and shakes his head. "Show her how it's done, Gaeton."

"Happily."

Shame makes my skin go hot and tight. I fucking love it. I love watching Beast's cock disappear into Gaeton's mouth even more. I start riding Gaeton as Beast fucks his mouth. It's messy and rough and I can't get enough. Each stroke rubs my clit against Gaeton, sends pleasure spiraling tighter and tighter through my body.

"She's close, Gaeton," Beast growls. "Cover her mouth so

everyone walking past this room doesn't know you're fucking her tight little pussy, that our little slut couldn't wait to be filled up with our come until tonight. She had to have it right this fucking second."

Gaeton's rough hand presses to my mouth, and I can't keep the moan inside. I don't know if it's that touch or Beast's words that send me over the edge. All I know is that I'm coming and it's perfect. Beneath me, Gaeton starts moving, fucking up into me. It's only when he curses low and hard as he orgasms that I realize Beast's not in his mouth any longer.

That's when Beast's words penetrate.

Our come.

Beast grabs my hips and lifts me off Gaeton's cock. My feet hit the ground and he bends me down over the chair, over our husband. The word thrills me. *Husband. Mine.*

And then Beast's cock is there, shoving into me from behind. I can't stop my moan. I don't even try. His exasperated curse almost makes me smile. "Her mouth, Gaeton. Keep her quiet."

Gaeton snags the back of my neck and then his mouth is on mine and his other hand is between my thighs, stroking my clit as Beast fucks me. I cling to his shoulders, as much to maintain our contact as to hold myself steady against Beast's thrusts. This is too good, too perfect, too dirty.

And then Beast goes and makes it more of everything.

He leans down over my back, his cock impossibly deep inside me. "You're going to walk into that reception with our come dripping down your thighs, little slut. A reminder of who you belong to." He nips the back of my neck just hard enough to hurt. "A sign of ownership. Your ours, and we're yours. Forever. Say it."

I break my kiss with Gaeton. "Yours. Forever."

"Who does this pussy belong to, little slut?"

"You." I meet Gaeton's hot gaze. "And you."

"That's right. *Ours.*" Beast's strokes get rougher as he nears the edge. And then he's coming, gripping my shoulder to hold me in place as he fills me up just like Gaeton did. I can't stop shivering from the pleasure sparking through me. He eases out of me and drops me back into Gaeton's lap. "Once more."

I blink up at him. "What?"

But Gaeton is already moving, lifting one of my legs up and wide and resuming stroking my clit in that lazy way of his, as if we have all the time in the world. I writhe against his chest as we watch Beast get dressed, but Gaeton never quite pushes me over the edge. I understand why when Beast motions with an impatient hand and Gaeton pushes me into his arms.

Beast turns me and urges me to brace myself against the dresser next to my dress. There's a mirror there, and we both watch Gaeton pull his tux back on as Beast fucks me with his fingers. "He looks good, doesn't he?"

"*Yes.*" I'm so close, I'm almost sobbing.

Beast holds me in place as he draws me closer and closer to the edge. There's no more teasing. He's intent on his destination, and he knows my body well enough to make it happen on his timeline. "Sometime at the reception, I want you to suck his cock. Get your lipstick all over him for me to find later. Do you understand me?"

"Yes," I whisper.

"Good girl."

And then I'm coming, my orgasm so intense it almost makes me black out. I'm vaguely aware of Beast catching me around the waist and Gaeton laughing as he comes to pull us both into his arms. We stand like that for what feels like a small eternity, me bracketed by them and their strength. Finally, I lift my head. "I love you both so much, it takes my breath away."

"You're mine. Forever."

"Forever," Gaeton and I say together. He kisses me and then leans over me to kiss Beast. "Here's to the first day of the rest of our lives. Come on. We have a party to get to."

11

SPARRING
GAETON

I dodge the punch aimed at my throat and dance back a step. "That was a cheap shot."

Beast wipes the sweat from his forehead with the back of his hand and gives me a wicked grin. "Anyone you fight outside the ring isn't going to play nice."

"Neither are you, apparently." I gauge his stance, waiting for the tell-tale movement of his hips to signal another strike. Some fighters signal their intentions with their eyes or shoulders, but Beast is too well-trained for that kind of rookie mistake. But even he can't go from stationary to attacking without some kind of tell.

The gym around us is empty, courtesy of our late-night workout. He hasn't been able to sleep well this week, not with the news coming out of Sabine Valley. Every time Isabelle or I bring it up, he shuts us down. Isabelle might be content to give him his space and let him work through whatever's going on in that pretty head of his, but that's now how I roll.

I lean forward on my toes and laugh when he tenses. "Almost got you."

"You know what they say about 'almost,' Gaeton."

Yeah, I do. Just like I know that this is exactly what he needs; work off some tension and then we're going to sit down and talk. The lack of communication is what fucked all three of us the first time, and there's no way in hell I'm willing to let us travel down those old roads.

Not even if Beast's ex, Cohen, is alive.

I move back a step, and Beast follows. The ring is the standard size, but it always feels smaller when I'm in here with him. He's too damn fast. I can't let my guard down for even a second. He's also patient enough to outlast me. That is, he's patient when I'm not in the mood to provoke him. I flick my fingers at him. "How about a friendly wager?"

His blue eyes narrow. "Only if you feel like offering something you're willing to lose."

"None of that bullshit." I grin. "Whoever wins gets to fuck the other...right here in the ring."

Beast goes so still, he doesn't seem to even breathe. "Risky. Someone could walk in."

"Yeah, they could." I start edging to one side, and he rotates to follow me without hesitation. "But the only person likely to interrupt is Isabelle, and she'll just join in." Though, really, Isabelle isn't going to interrupt. She's been running herself ragged trying to keep up with her sisters. Our woman is all-in for the territory, but she's not used to the amount of energy required. She'll find her feet eventually, but add in her worry about Beast and she's exhausted. Tonight we stayed long enough to get her mind off things and wait for her to fall asleep before coming here. She won't wake until morning. Hopefully by then, I'll be able to tell her honestly that we have nothing to worry about with Beast.

"You're on." He comes at me before I have a chance to

brace, and I barely block his punches and kicks before they make contact with my torso. The fucker is *fast*, and he fights dirty, even in sparring.

That's okay.

I fight dirty, too.

I count off in my head. When Beast is exhausted and distracted, like he is now, he falls into a pattern. Punch, punch, kick. When he tries to kick my thigh, I grab his ankle and yank, toppling him to the ground. I follow him to the ground, barely catching his shoulders before he rolls out of the way. I use my larger size to try to pin him.

It's like trying to pin down water. We're both sweaty and panting and I'm going to be covered in bruises tomorrow. He will be, too. Beast almost gets out from under me, but like I said—I play dirty.

I kiss him.

Just like that, pent up aggression turns to pure desire. He stops trying to get away and digs his hands into my hair, holding me as he takes my mouth. My cock was already semi-hard thinking about the stakes, and I groan against him as I go rock hard. Our loose shorts are barely a barrier between us. If anything, they allow my cock to slide alongside his even easier.

I break away enough to say. "After this, we're talking."

Beast hesitates the barest fraction of a second. "Yeah. Okay."

Thank fuck. I brace myself on my elbows and thrust against him. "You're pinned, motherfucker."

His grin makes my stomach do a little flip like I'm at the top of a roller coaster and about to slip into a freefall. Beast tows me back down. "Yeah, I am."

I want to sink into the kiss, to just make-out like a pair of horny teenagers for a bit, but I need him too much. Still, it's harder to pull away than it should be. Even after nearly a year together, I can't get enough of him. "Don't move."

Beast props himself up on his elbows and watches me climb out of the ring and walk to the bag I brought with us. His brows inch up when I return with a bottle of lube. "Someone's prepared."

"Fighting and fucking, Beast. I figured we wouldn't have a proper conversation until we'd managed one or the other —or both."

He grimaces a little. "Pushy."

"It's been a week of this shit. I'm entitled to be pushy." I sink to my knees between his thighs and hook my hands into the waistband of his shorts. "You want it rough."

It wasn't a question, but he's already nodding. "I *need* it rough right now."

I almost ask for his safe word, but this is less about boundary-crossing kink than about driving out the demons riding him. I know where Beast's line is, just like he knows where mine is. There might be times when we dance on those lines, but tonight isn't one of them.

Instead, I toss his shorts to the side and grab his arm. It's easy to flip him onto his stomach because he's already rolling with the motion and going onto his hands and knees. I smooth my hands down his scarred back and squeeze his ass. I spread lube over my cock and down his ass and then start to work my way slowly into him. No matter how rough he wants it, I want this good for him rather than another way to flog himself over the shit going on in his head right now.

I'm halfway into his ass when he drops his head between his shoulders. "*Fuck.*"

"This is what you need, isn't it?" I grip his hip and sink another few inches. "A reminder of whose rings are on your finger right now." Damn it, maybe *I* needed this, too. A year ago, when I asked Beast what would happen if his ex really was alive, I didn't honestly believe it could be possible. Beast was *so sure* Cohen had died. He'd mourned him.

Now we find out the bastard has been alive this whole time.

I finally sheath myself completely and lean over his back to brace one hand on the other side of his. I kiss the back of his neck, his skin salty with his sweat, and set my teeth against him. "He can't have you. Do you fucking hear me, Beast? You're ours and he made his choices when he didn't come to Carver City." I start moving slowly, and then picking up pace when he moans. Each word punctuated by a thrust. "You. Are. Ours."

"I know!" He bursts out. "Fuck, you think I don't know that?"

I grab the lube and pause long enough to coat my palm. I reach around his hip and wrap my fist around his cock. "How would I know? You haven't said a single fucking word." I meant to hold off on this conversation until we were finished fucking, but we really do communicate better when we're fucking. Twelve months hasn't changed that.

"This cock." I squeeze him roughly, earning another moan. "This ass." A rough thrust. "Mine. Isabelle's. Fucking *say it*."

Beast shoves back against me. "I'm yours. Now fuck me properly."

I pump slowly, timing the strokes of my hand to coincide. Teasing him. I didn't realized how pissed I am about his withdrawal until this moment. "Do you know what it's been like watching you retreat? Isabelle is about to lose her fucking mind, and I can't comfort her because *I'm* not sure of you right now. I haven't been since Lammas night." Since

Beast got a call from an old contact in Sabine Valley informing him that all seven of the Paine brothers are alive and well, including his ex.

Beast exhales slowly, like he's fighting for control right along with me. "I love you and Isabelle, Gaeton. I *chose* you back in your apartment during that week, and I *chose* you again at the altar six months ago. Cohen being alive doesn't change that." He curses when I give his cock a few rough strokes. "I haven't said anything, because I didn't know how I felt. I mourned that fucker, and now I find out he's been alive this entire time and never reached out? I'm pissed and I'm fucking *hurt*, but none of that means I want anything different than what I have."

Relief makes me dizzy. In my heart of hearts, I knew he wasn't going to leave us, but the longer we went without talking about it, the more fear took root. I grab one of his hands and guide it to his cock. "Make yourself come while I fuck your ass."

He doesn't hesitate, stroking himself even more roughly than I had been. I lean back and grip his hips. He asked for a rough fucking, and apparently that's exactly what we both need. I drive into him, cursing as how good this feels now that I can focus entirely on the pleasure without the fear lingering in the back of my mind.

Beast growls my name as he orgasms, and I let myself follow him over the edge, barely pulling out in time to come across his back. It feels like marking him as mine all over again, and the sight soothes something dark deep inside me. "Don't move."

He huffs out a laugh. "Wasn't planning on it."

I yank up my pants and climb out of the ring again to grab two towels. After I get our mess cleaned up, I pass him his shorts and wait while he pulls them back on. Only when we're both clothed do I speak again, "The whole point of being in a relationship is that you can talk through shit. I get that it's not any more natural for you than it is for either me or Isabelle, but we need that. You closed us out and it wasn't okay."

He scrubs a hand over his face. "Yeah, I know. I just needed time. I still need time."

"Then tell us that."

"You've gotten damn good at this communication shit."

"It's a work in progress." I grab his hand and pull him to his feet. "Think you can manage some sleep after we shower?"

He gives me a tired smile. "Yeah. I actually feel better now."

"Weird how that works."

"Oh, fuck off." He laughs hoarsely, but the sound fades almost as soon as it begins. "Look, I'm sorry I freaked you out. I'm all twisted up, and it didn't even register that you wouldn't realize I have no intention of walking away. Cohen made his choice, just like I've made mine." He frowns at the floor of the ring. "I have some fucking questions about what the hell he was thinking, but in the end it doesn't really matter. I have you and Isabelle, and I'm better off."

I really, really want to agree with him that it doesn't matter, but I suspect it's not the truth. I take a deep breath and strive to drown out the fear. "It might help if you talked to him. To get answers, I mean."

Beast looks at me for a long time. "That took a lot for you to offer."

No point in denying it. "Yeah."

He moves, quicker than he has right to, and hooks the back of my neck. He tows me down and kisses me hard. I barely have a chance to sink into it before he pulls back a little. "Maybe I'll decide at some point that I want to talk to him, but I'm not there." He massages the back of my neck a little. "If I decide that's something I need, I'll talk about it with you and Isabelle before I do anything."

I exhale slowly, trying not to let my relief show. "That's all we ask."

He kisses me one last time and then releases me. "I love you, Gaeton. Never fucking doubt *that*."

"I don't." It's the truth. I don't have a single doubt about how Beast feels for me. Not anymore. It doesn't mean life isn't complicated, though.

He ducks out of the ring and holds the ropes for me to follow him. He doesn't speak again until we reach the door and step out into the hallway. "How tired are you?"

Only one answer to that. "What do you have in mind?"

His grin is downright wicked. "Figure I have some making up to do with Isabelle. Want to help?"

I answer with a grin of my own. "As if you have to ask. The answer is always, will always be *fuck yes*."

THIS SHORT ORIGINALLY APPEARED AS the June 2020 short for my Patreon. Each month, patrons nominate their favorite couples and characters, vote on one, and I write a brand new short featuring the winner. For more bonus stories, please consider joining my Patreon.

COHEN'S STORY will continue in the Sabine Valley Series, starting with Abel.

12

SEVEN MINUTES IN HEAVEN
GAETON

"She tell you what's up?"

I glance at Beast. He doesn't look overly concerned, but why would he be? Isabelle just told us to meet her at my apartment at seven for a surprise. She's done this a few times over the last few months, and the end result is always a good thing for everyone. It makes me glad I kept this place; a spot for us to fuck around that isn't in Isabelle's family's home. "Nope."

Beast rolls his shoulders the same way he does before a fight. I don't exactly blame him for it. Life's kicked him in the teeth enough times that even now, even with us, part of him is always expecting the worst. He doesn't let that fear sabotage our shit, though, and that's all we can really ask of him.

I open the door and, with a smirk, walk through ahead of him. The first thing I hear are giggles in two distinct voices. I grin back at Beast and then bellow. "Honey, we're home!"

Isabelle walks out of the bedroom, tugging Aurora behind her. They don't look like they've been up to no good; more like they're *about to*. Isabelle's wearing one of the new dresses she bought last week, a short black number that makes her tits look amazing and flicks around her thighs with every step. Aurora's clothes look like maybe they started out as a school uniform, but someone took a pair of scissors to them. She's tied her white shirt beneath her breasts and the skirt is barely long enough cover the essentials.

Isabelle hurries to me and gives me a kiss, slipping out of my arms before I can settle into it, and gives Beast the same treatment. "Right on time."

I cross my arms over my chest and give the women a mock serious look. "Did you start the party without us?"

Aurora presses her hand to her chest and gives me an innocent look. "Would we do that?"

"Yes."

She laughs. "You're right; we totally would. But we didn't this time."

Isabelle takes both my hand and Beast's and leads us into the living room. It looks like someone decided to have a slumber party with the space covered in pillows and blankets. I eye the space as she tugs us down to sit on either side of her. "We have a perfectly good bed in the next room over. Why are we sitting on the floor?"

She gives another of those laughs that sounds so fucking happy, I swear my heart grows three sizes. "We're going to play Seven Minutes in Heaven."

"If it's only seven minutes, someone is doing something wrong," Beast says.

Isabelle shakes her head. "Come on, you know what I'm talking about right? Didn't you ever play this game in high school?"

Beast and I exchange a look. Neither of us had what a person could call a traditional high school experience, and we'd both had bigger things to worry about than attending parties in some kid's basement. "No."

"Never."

She sighs and looks at Aurora. "I knew it. We're going to have to show them the ropes."

I'm not sure why she's decided that this is the route she wants to take tonight, but I'm willing to play. I slouch back against the couch and stretch my legs out. "What are the rules?"

Aurora sits primly in the spot across from Isabelle. "Normally, the two people involved go into a closet or something and make-out for seven minutes while everyone giggles and speculates about them." She smiles slowly. "But we're not teenagers, so Isabelle decided to make it more interesting."

Isabelle picks up right where she left off. "No closets. We do it out in the open." She's practically vibrating with excitement. "Anything goes for the seven-minute duration." She pulls a bottle out from beneath the pillow next to her. "This is how we pick."

"Anything goes..."

She huffs. "Yes, Gaeton, Aurora and I have our established safe words, and if you and Beast change your mind, we can stop."

I grab the bottle from her. "Fuck like that's going to happen. Let's do this." How many movies have I seen with Spin the Bottle and this kind of shit in it? It always seemed like that kind of thing happened in another world. I don't care that I didn't experience it as a teenager. This shit is a thousand times better. I set the bottle in the open space on the floor in the middle of us and give it a spin.

It lands on Isabelle.

She wastes no time crawling into my lap. "Set the timer, Aurora." And then she's kissing me, all soft and sweet and so fucking perfect. There are still days when I wake up, half sure that this is all a fever dream, that only in my fantasies am I really allowed to call Beast and Isabelle mine in truth. Moments like these have it all rushing back to me. She's mine. He's mine. This is really happening.

I slide my hands up Isabelle's thighs and grip her ass, urging her to grind against me. As if we're really just teenagers making out. It's tempting to escalate things, but I kind of like the idea of playing the slow game, of dialing up the heat in seven-minute increments until we all lose control.

All too soon, Aurora says, "Time."

Isabelle lifts her head. Her lips are plumped from our kiss and she's breathing just as raggedly as I am. She gives one last agonizing roll of her hips, rubbing herself against where my cock is trying to burst out of my pants, and then crawls back to her spot.

She spins the bottle, and it lands on Aurora. Beast and I exchange another look, and I can't read the expression on his face. He's turned on, sure, but there's something else there beneath the surface. He says, "Time starts now."

Isabelle practically tackles Aurora to the ground. Aurora's played with us on a semi-regular basis since that first night, and it's always like this with them. They go at it like they might never get another chance again, like one of us will step in and stop them if they don't hurry it up. Since that's a fantasy we've played out more than few times, I can't really blame them.

And it's one hell of a show.

Aurora's got her hands up Isabelle's dress within the first minute, and she's got Isabelle coming all over her fingers right as Beast says, "Time."

And so it goes. Aurora lands on Beast, and spends the

entire seven minutes in a battle of wills with him while she sucks his cock. He wins. He lands on Isabelle. Isabelle lands on me—and my cock—I land on Aurora. Aurora gets a second shot at Beast.

Somewhere along the way, we start losing clothes. My shirt is long-gone. So is Aurora's shirt. Both her and Isabelle lost their panties early on. Even Beast hasn't bothered to shove his hard cock back into his pants after Isabelle spent seven minutes riding him.

And then his spin lands on me.

I don't hesitate to crawl to him. I fucking love the way he watches me, his eyes blazing with pleasure and his dominant side barely kept on a leash. I don't stop until I'm looming over him on my hands and knees, our faces even. "Hey."

"Hey." His voice has deepened with pleasure.

"Begin," murmurs Isabelle. I glance over to find her hand under her dress, working herself with her fingers as she watches us.

It gives me an idea.

I lean down and drag my mouth over Beast's neck. He tenses beneath me, but allows me to work my way up to his ear. "What do you say we change the game?" I murmur.

"Yes." He turns his head and lays one hell of a kiss on me. Beast always takes my mouth as if he owns me, because he sure as fuck does, and this time is no exception. He kisses me until my arms are shaking and it's everything I can do not to drop on top of him and grind away until I come all over his stomach. Then his hand finds my chest and he presses me lightly back. "Now."

We move as a coordinated unit. I shove off him and snag Aurora around the waist, and Beast grabs Isabelle's ankle and drags her over to him, crawling between her thighs. She gives a surprised laugh that turns into a throaty moan, and I know his cock has found her pussy.

For her part, Aurora settles in my lap easily with a sweet smile. "What's on the menu, big guy?"

We've played out Isabelle's fantasy of Beast and I fucking Aurora a few times, enough to know exactly where the boundaries are. It's blatant that tonight it's on the menu, as Aurora says. Still, I have an idea to take things to the next level. "Is your pussy feeling needy, Aurora?"

"Always."

"Guess we better fill it up, then."

Her grin widens. "We were hoping you'd say that." She reaches past me and pulls a condom out from between the cushions of the couch.

I raise my brows. "You and Isabelle really thought of everything, huh? You're like kinky Boy Scouts."

"I've fucked enough former Boy Scouts to know those assholes are all kinky." She rips open the condom and waits while I shove down my pants to roll it over my cock. I don't give her a chance to get settled; I just lift both myself and her up onto the couch and turn her around so she's strad-dling me, facing Beast and Isabelle. Only then do I let her work herself down my cock. It feels fucking good. It's going to feel better.

I grip Aurora's hips, keeping us sealed together, and say, "Beast." I don't have to elaborate. I never do with him, not anymore.

He doesn't answer me with words. He simply pulls out of Isabelle, yanks her dress over her head, and hauls her to us. She ends up on her hands and knees between my and Auro-ra's spread thighs, Beast at her back. I don't have to say a damn thing. Isabelle dives for Aurora's pussy even as Beast thrusts into her. I feel the moment her mouth makes contact with Aurora's clit because Aurora clenches around me. "Fuck."

"Don't lose it," Beast growls.

"*You* don't lose it." I speak through gritted teeth. Aurora is making little movements on my cock, grinding herself down as Isabelle tongues her clit. I don't have a good enough view, so I dig my hand into Aurora's blue hair and tug her back to press against my chest. It lets me look down her body to where Isabelle has her skirt shoved up. The sheer happiness on my woman's face nearly has me orgasming on the spot. That and the way Beast grips her hips and thrusts into her in short, brutal strokes. She's moaning and Aurora is whimpering and, fuck, this is one of the better surprises Isabelle has put together.

Aurora comes with a cry loud enough that it's almost a scream. Beast is already moving, jerking Isabelle back and reversing our positions. I keep Aurora on my cock as I follow them to the floor, using my hold in her hair to guide her face between Isabelle's legs. She goes eagerly. Of course she does.

Beast and I keep going, giving it to them until they're so fucking limp from pleasure that they can barely keep up. Only then does he meet my gaze and nod. Fucking *finally*. I grab Aurora's hips and pound into her. I've been on edge for so long, it takes nothing at all to send me flying. Pressure builds and then I'm coming hard, watching Beast do the same.

It takes several long minutes before I have enough control of my body to get up and dispose of the condom. I come back to find Isabelle cuddling up in the blankets next to Beast and grabbing the remote. She gives me a slow smile. "These parties always end with movie. It's an unspoken rule."

We all need time to come down after that, so I nod.

"Works for me." I end up between Aurora and Beast. Isabelle practically drapes herself over all three of us, and we settle in to watch the slasher she picked out. Aurora leans against me and idly braids Isabelle's hair, while Beast is a solid presence pressed against my other side.

I take Isabelle's hand and press a kiss to her knuckles. "This was one hell of a surprise."

"I know." She sounds half asleep. "I'll have to get creative to come up with something better."

I share a look with Beast. We really are lucky fuckers, aren't we? I grin. "We can't wait."

THIS SHORT ORIGINALLY APPEARED AS the October 2020 short for my Patreon. Each month, patrons nominate their favorite couples and characters, vote on one, and I write a brand new short featuring the winner. For more bonus stories, please consider joining my Patreon.

13

LADIES' NIGHT IN CARVER CITY

AURORA

"I'm going to invite her."

Meg sighs and I can practically feel her reluctant amusement before she speaks. "You don't have to bring every single person under your wing, Aurora."

She *would* see it that way. That's how Meg operates, after all. No matter how aggravated she'll get if I point it out, she gathers people to her. Hades makes the deals, but Meg is the glue that holds this place together. Every single submissive and Dominant on staff would happily throw themselves in front of a bullet for her, myself included.

I can only take care of myself, and even then it's a struggle at times.

I turn and look at her. She's leaning against the bar, as at ease as always. Tonight she's wearing a pair of pants that are tight enough to be a second skin and a complex black matching bra under an oversized silk button-down shirt that *almost* looks like she stole it from Hercules's closet. She catches me looking and smirks. "We're not having that kind of fun tonight."

My cheeks heat and I laugh. "Can't blame me for looking."

Meg shakes her head. "Focus. Inviting Jasmine along means dealing with Jafar. Are you prepared for *that?*"

"You say it like he's a big scary monster." There was a time when Jafar played with a variety of submissives at the club, including me, but these days he only has eyes for his woman. It's really, really sweet, though I'm smart enough to never say that in front of him. The man practically walks around with hearts in his eyes, but he's still one of the scarier people in Carver City.

"I say it like he's Jafar." She chuckles. "But if you're not going to change your mind, let's get this over with."

"You like Jasmine."

"Of course I like Jasmine." She gives me a wicked grin. "I also like pulling on Jafar's tail. I just wanted to make sure *you* were ready for it."

It shouldn't rankle that Meg underestimates me, even after all this time. I spent years cultivating a persona that inspires those around me to protect, because I wasn't strong enough to protect myself. It's my own fault that the skin doesn't fit well anymore. I'm making changes, but it stands to reason that it will take longer for others to recognize the difference in me. "I'm ready."

"Then, by all means." She motions an elegant hand to the booth tucked in the corner. It's become Jasmine and Jafar's customary spot when they spend time in the Underworld. Sometimes Meg joins them, but they tend to stick to themselves. Hence us inviting her along for girl's night.

I have to lengthen my stride to keep up with Meg. It feels weird to be wearing shoes in the lounge—not to mention actual clothes—but I push the feelings aside. I'm on a mission.

Jasmine looks up as we come to a stop by the table. She's really, really pretty. Long black hair, flawless medium-brown skin, and big brown eyes. She smiles at Meg. "It's been a long time."

Meg shrugs a single shoulder. "You two should get out more. It's been long enough. Your power base is solidified. Live a little."

Jasmine raises her brows. "I really like you, Meg, but keep your nose out of our territory's business." There it is, the sliver of coldness that all the powerful people in Carver City exhibit. When Jasmine took over her father's territory, it raised a few questions about if she'd be able to hold it. But it's been over a year now and she's showing no signs of buckling.

I bounce on my toes a little. "What Meg is *trying* to say is that we're going out for a lady's night with Allecto and Tink tonight, and we'd like you to come with us." I hold up a hand before either she or Jafar can speak. "Both Hades and Hook have people at the bar we're going to—which is in neutral territory—but we're more than happy to have a few of your security people join. We're not being reckless."

Jasmine glances at Jafar. He doesn't look particularly happy about this offer, but he manages to dredge up a smile. "It's your choice."

She considers me. "I don't know you outside of reputation."

Meg starts to speak, but I nudge her with my shoulder. "Look, all the territory business in Carver City can be really isolating. We thought it'd be nice to spend some time getting to know each other, and maybe be friends."

"Friends."

"Sure, friends." I give her a sunny smile.

She gives me a look like she's not sure if I'm joking or

not, but finally shrugs. "Yes, I'll come." She leans over and presses a quick kiss to Jafar's lips. "I'll make it up to you."

He leans back, amusement lingering in his dark eyes. "I'm sure you will. Give me a few moments." He slides out of the booth and walks toward the hallway leading to Hades's public office.

Jasmine motions for us to slide into the booth. She looks a bit like a queen with her subjects, and I glance at Meg to see if that will irritate her. If there's a queen of the Underworld, it's *her*. Meg seems just as amused as Jafar. "How have you been?"

"Good. Tired, but good." Jasmine smiles. "Things are going well."

"You and Jafar seem to have figured a few things out." She nods, and I follow her gaze to the ring on Jasmine's finger. I hadn't even noticed it. It's delicate and reasonably sized, but even I can tell that it's custom made for her. I try to imagine what it would be like to have someone love you enough—*know* you enough—to create a custom engagement ring. It boggles the mind.

Jasmine holds up her hand and looks at the ring. "I proposed."

"Good for you."

"There you are!"

We turn and look as Allecto and Tink walk up. Tink is, as always, too fucking cute. She's styled her blond hair into something resembling a crown and she is wearing a pair of cut-off shorts and a graphic T-shirt that looks faded and soft. Her shoes are strappy and the heels appear sharp enough to stab someone in the heart. Next to her, Allecto is wearing a variation of her normal outfit—dark jeans and a dark purple tank top with boots that I have no doubt are steel-toed. Allecto likes to be prepared for anything.

Tink props her hands on her hips. "So, are you coming or what?"

"Yes, I'll join you."

"Good, then let's get going." She glances around the room. "Hook made some dire comments about me being on my best behavior, and while I kind of doubt he'll crash ladies' night, I also wouldn't put it past him to show up and drag me off somewhere semi-dark." Her sharp grin goes a little dreamy.

Something like jealousy sinks barbs into my chest. I am so incredibly happy that my friends have found happiness, but a small part of me can't help that I also feel bad about it. They have something I don't know if I'll ever have. How can I? I'd have to let someone close enough to touch my heart, and I've long since grown a carefully curated wall of thorns around it. Friends are risk enough. But loving someone? It hurts too much to lose them. I don't ever want to feel that way again.

Jafar strides up. He gives Tink and Allecto a quick business-like once-over and turns his attention on Jasmine. "Two of our men will meet you at the elevator. They'll bring you home once you're done."

"See, that wasn't hard at all." She rises and he pulls her into his arms and lays a kiss on her that has all of us groaning dramatically.

Then Jafar is gone, stalking across the room and disappearing out the door. From the look on Jasmine's face, she's considering changing plans and following him, but she gives herself a shake and smiles at us. "Where are we headed?"

We end up at a bar down the street. Hades and Allecto don't like us to wander far. We've all learned the hard way that neutral territory only really matters to the people in

Carver City. Outsiders don't respect our rules, which makes them dangerous. It's a small risk, but Allecto is head of security because she considers all variables, no matter how unlikely. We trust her for the same reason.

Not to mention she'd mow down any threat the second it arose. She's badass like that.

I sidle up to the bar next to her and nudge her with my shoulder. "You look tense."

"I always look tense."

"You know what will help with that." I waggle my eyebrows.

Allecto gives me a severe look, but it doesn't quite stick because her lips curve. "So help me, if you say shots and karaoke—"

"Shots and karaoke!"

She motions the bartender. "I'll do both on one condition."

I already know what's coming, just like she knew what I was about to suggest. We've known each other a really long time at this point, and we've gone through this song and dance... a lot. I huff out a breath. "If you're about to say extra sparring sessions..."

"Extra sparring sessions." She gives me a sharp grin. "You're spending so much time fucking, you're getting rusty. I kicked your ass the last two times."

"You kicked my ass because you're an ass-kicking queen."

"That's also true." She orders a round of shots and then turns back to me while the bartender gets to work pouring them. "But it doesn't change the fact that you're slacking."

Combat training wasn't really part of my deal with Hades, but like working as a submissive, it's something I've started doing over the years. One more ridiculous way I can trick myself into feeling more in control, more like I won't really follow in my mother's footsteps. Our situations are nothing alike, but if she'd known how to fight, maybe she wouldn't have ended up in a decades' long coma. Maybe she'd still be *her*, still be able to hug and smile and follow the fierce ambition that is barely more than a faded memory for me. It might even be imagined. I was so young when she was injured, I barely remember the person she used to be at all. I only have my grandmother's stories.

"Aurora." Allecto taps the spot between my eyebrows. "Three times this week."

"Three extra practices for three karaoke songs."

She sighs, but she's still smiling. "You drive a hard bargain."

"I learned from the best."

"Yeah, I guess you did." She shakes her head. "You have yourself a deal."

I'll regret it when she's sending me flying across the mat, but right now it makes me happy. Allecto doesn't let down her guard often, so when she does, it's a really treat. Tonight is going to be so much *fun*.

It starts with a round of shots. And then another. I'm delighted to find out that Jasmine is a bit of a lightweight, and that she's rather bratty when she's not guarding her words. She and Tink verbally spar while Allecto croons out one of my favorite karaoke songs of all time.

Meg throws an arm around my shoulder and gives me a squeeze. "You were right. We all needed this tonight. And it was a good idea to invite Jasmine along."

I give her a long look, trying not to grin. "Are you drunk?" Meg *never* drinks enough to get drunk. Or if she does, I've only seen it once or twice in nearly ten years. Tonight's special, indeed.

"Of course not. How gauche." She laughs. "I'm simply enjoying myself."

The bar's lights flicker on, signaling last call. I groan, and then groan some more when the door opens up and Hercules, Hook, and Jafar stride into the bar. They must have been waiting in a line outside, which strikes me as particularly hilarious. All those big, brawny men waiting to give their women the maximum time for fun before they come collect them. I'm not even sure those three *like* each other, but they move almost as a unit, dividing and zeroing in on their partners.

Jafar scoops up Jasmine and gives her a downright indulgent smile. "Have fun?"

"Yes." She grins at him. "Let's fuck in the car."

"Let's see how you feel in a few minutes." He turns without another word and heads out the door.

Hook doesn't pick up Tink, but he does slide an arm around her waist and steer her for the door. He shoots a happy smile over his shoulder at us. "Looks like you all had a good time."

"The best time!" I realize I'm shouting and clamp my hand over my mouth.

Meg's laughter cuts off when Hercules hauls her off her feet. He winks at me and then they're gone, following Hook and Tink out the door.

Allecto ambles up. As always, it doesn't matter how many shots she takes, she never gets sloppy. The only indication that she's feeling the alcohol is how easy she grins at me. "Singles last."

"Don't remind me." It just slips out. I frown at my feet. They really hurt. These heels look great, but they definitely aren't for dancing. "Not that I care. I like being single."

"Uh huh, Aurora. Sure you do." She loops an arm around my shoulders and steers us for the door.

The walk back to the Underworld seems to take forever, the street stretching like taffy beneath my feet. I blink. "Shit, I'm drunk."

"I know." She laughs, the bitch.

"I hate you."

"No you don't." Another of those laughs. "But you will tomorrow."

Right. The sparring. Damn it, I really don't want to do it. No matter how good I get, I'll never be on Allecto's level, and she barely pulls her punches. Something about it not providing a real enough experience to cut down on my reaction time. It made more sense when I didn't have alcohol flowing through my veins, giving everything a warm, fuzzy feel. "Maybe we should fuck."

Allecto snorts. "Yeah, no."

"Why not?"

"One, you're drunk as a skunk. Two, we're friends, and while you fuck your friends, I don't." She gives my shoulders a squeeze. "You're just feeling lonely after watching everyone couple up. Don't let it go to your head."

"Stop telling me my life."

"Then stop hitting on me just because I'm a warm body."

I open my mouth and my brain finally catches up to my tongue. "I hit on you because you're hot."

"I'm hot and I always tell you no."

That surprises a laugh out of me. We're almost back to the Underworld, back to something resembling reality. "I'll stop, I promise. Sorry."

"Nah, it's all good." She shoulders open the door and tows me through it. "You're cute when you're all drunk and flirty. It's endearing. Like a puppy."

"*Ouch.*" I press my hands to my chest and weave my way to the elevators. "A shot to the heart."

"Something tells me you'll survive it." She follows me into the elevator, still grinning. "Let's get you back to your room before you face-plant and I have to explain to Hades how I let his precious Aurora break her pretty nose."

"Eh." I wave that away. "He won't care."

"Sure he won't. Because Hades definitely doesn't get overprotective and growly when it comes to you." I don't know what my expression is doing, but she bursts out laughing. "Like I said."

I am too focused on putting one foot in front of the other to respond until we reach my door and Allecto keys it open. I slump against the doorframe. "Hey, Allecto."

"Yeah?"

"I'm really glad we're friends. Like... really glad. You're pretty awesome."

Her grin softens. "You're pretty awesome yourself, Aurora. Now get your ass to bed and don't be late tomorrow. If I have to come looking for you, I'll haul your ass into a cold shower and then you won't be glad we're friends."

I gasp, but I can't keep my mock outrage. I'm still laughing as I shut the door and stumble my way to bed. It doesn't matter that I'm single. I *like* being single. I'll even remember that tomorrow, once the alcohol has faded out of my system. I'll remember that I'm not actually lonely. I'll remember that I have purpose. I'll remember that I'm really, really happy.

Tomorrow.

Yeah, I'll remember all that tomorrow.

∾

THIS SHORT ORIGINALLY APPEARED AS the July 2020 short for my Patreon. Each month, patrons nominate their favorite couples and characters, vote on one, and I write a brand new short featuring the winner. For more bonus stories, please consider joining my Patreon.

14

HONEY, WE'RE HOME
ZURIELLE

"Y ou've done well, Zuri."

I smile at Ursa. In the months since my auction, since I fell in love with Ursa and Alaric for real, she's slowly started bringing me along when she goes to meetings and walking me through the backside of her operations. Ursa runs a tight ship. But then, do I expect anything different?

I lean my head on her shoulder as the car cuts through Carver City, heading back to her penthouse. "Thank you."

She takes my hand and traces the lines in my palms with a single nail. "There's nothing to thank me for."

I hide my smile. "I know it hasn't been that long, and you're letting me see the details of something that's important to you. I know that means something."

Her finger pauses its tracing for a moment and then resumes. "I love you, little Zurielle. Of course I'm letting you in."

But there's no *of course* about it. If I've learned anything, it's that you can take nothing for granted in this life. Not safety, not stability, certainly not love. She's given me the gift of all three. Her and Alaric. It's also clear that she's still uncomfortable with my pointing out her willing vulnerability.

I close my hand over hers. "Your people will walk through fire for you."

"Yes."

"It's a sign of a good leader."

She laughs. "If you don't treat your people well and give them a reason to feel loyal to you, you can expect a knife in the back the first chance they get. I've seen it happen enough times to learn from others' mistakes. To learn from *my* mistake."

"Have you thought about opening up some kind of trade with Sabine Valley?"

Ursa leans back and lifts her arm, an invitation to shift closer that I'm only too happy to take. She looks down at me, her red lips curved. "You've been talking with Alaric."

Yes, but not about trade. I'm intensely curious about Sabine Valley because of how different it seems from both Olympus and Carver City. "He *does* have a connection there, especially now that his cousins have regained some level of power. A trade agreement might benefit both them and us. No one else from Carver City has anything like that set up."

She smooths my hair back and tucks it behind my ear. "Malone has more than enough connections to that city to have set something up."

Because she's an Amazon, a member of one of the other factions. "But even if she has, there's still opportunity there." Doubt threatens to creep in. I thought it was a good idea, but now I'm not so sure. "Don't you think?"

Ursa opens her mouth, seems to reconsider, and finally

nods. "You're not wrong that there's a chance to use Alaric's connections to our advantage. We'll speak with him about setting up a meeting with one of his cousins."

That perks me up. "We?"

"It was your idea, Zuri. Of course you'll attend." She leans down and presses a light kiss to my lips. "I've never had anything resembling a partner. It will take some getting used to. Have patience with me."

"Of course." My heart feels like it might burst out of pure joy. I still can't quite believe that this is my life now, that I'm doing things I never dared dream. When I was young and used to imagine what my happily ever after might look like, something like this—in a relationship with the Sea Witch and Alaric. That there would be love and respect. That I would be stronger than I ever dared dream. I look out the window as we turn into the parking garage.

We're home.

Ursa and I make our way up to the penthouse, and her hand finds mine in the elevator. She gives me a squeeze. "I have half a dozen meetings next week. I'd like you at all of them."

Surprise and happy pleasure warm my chest. "Really?"

"Yes." She glances at me, her lips still curved in that small, satisfied smile. "If you want to become my second-in-command, you have to learn the ropes, and that won't happen if I keep you confined to the penthouse." For a moment, something like doubt lingers in her eyes. "Unless you don't want to..."

"I do!" I throw myself into her arms and press a hard kiss to her lips. It smears her lipstick, which means it's smeared mine, too, but I don't care. "You really mean it."

She wraps her arms around me. "I really mean it. You've

got a good head for this stuff, and you might be sweet with me, but you're already learning to be hard when it counts."

"I'll always be sweet with you," I whisper.

"I hope so." She kisses me and I lose myself in her taste, in the softness of her body against mine. The elevator ding as we reach the penthouse floor is an unwelcome interruption.

The smell that wafts through the doors as they open, on the other hand, is incredibly welcome. My stomach growls and Ursa laughs. "Let's get you fed before you expire on the spot."

"It's not that bad.'"

"Even so, darling." She takes my hand and tugs me after her.

The good smells get stronger as we walk through the entrance and down the hall to the kitchen. There we find Alaric monitoring something on the stove. To my delight, he's wearing the apron I jokingly bought him last week. It's frilly and pink and has *Kiss the Cook* written across the chest.

He turns as we enter the room and grins at us. There's a smear of some kind of sauce on his cheek and flour on both apron and his pants, but he looks downright delighted. "I've finally nailed it this time."

"If it tastes as good as it smells, you definitely have." Ursa leans in and gives him a quick kiss and then moves past him. "How long until it's ready?"

"Um." He gives the pot a dubious look. "Maybe ten minutes?"

"I'm going to change." She gives my hand one last squeeze and releases me. Then she's gone, sweeping out the door and down the hall toward our room.

I go up onto my toes and kiss Alaric. "Hey."

"Hey." He loops an arm around my waist. "How'd it go?"

It's impossible to keep my happy smile to myself. I beam up at him. "Really, really well. Ursa mentioned maybe me being her second-in-command."

He gives me an indulgent look and stirs the pot with a wooden spoon. "You know that was the plan all along. Why are you so surprised?"

"Honestly? I thought she might change her mind once I started shadowing her." It's not so easy to shuck off an entire lifetime's worth of being told how fragile and incompetent I am. Of being shielded from any and all darkness. Even though I know better, I half expect Ursa to decide to toss me into the penthouse and keep me there.

Alaric pulls me closer and rests his chin on my head. "You know better."

"Yeah, I guess I do." It doesn't stop the sheer burst of happiness that almost has me wiggling with glee. I tap his chest and peer into the pot. "Is that soup or sauce?"

"Zuri," he warns.

"It's an innocent question." I smile sweetly at him. "At least the smoke alarms aren't going off this time and you haven't set anything on fire."

He gives me a mock glare. "Maybe you're brilliant at everything you try the first time, but the rest of us mere mortals tend to misstep along the way."

I run my hands up his chest. "I'm just teasing."

"I know." He gives me a little nudge. "Go change. Dinner will be ready soon." Alaric glances at the pot. "Hopefully."

"I have the utmost faith in you."

Fifteen minutes later, we're all sitting around the table and eating the soup Alaric prepared. It *is* good. I look at Ursa and Alaric and...

I still can't quite believe that this is real. That I get to have both of these incredible people in my life and in my bed and that it's *working*. It might not be what I once thought I wanted, but it's a thousand times better than anything I could have dreamed up.

They're mine and I'm theirs and I wouldn't have it any other way.

15

HERCULES'S APOLOGY

HADES

"I have simple rules, Hercules." I sit at my desk and press my steepled fingers to my lips. Meg is at my shoulder as she always is these days, especially during meetings affecting the vital foundations of the Underworld. Foundations that include the obedience of my staff. Foundations that include the safety of my patrons.

Hercules sits stiffly in the chair in front of the desk, his strong jaw set in a stubborn line I recognize all too well. Normally, he's a natural fit in the position we've found for him. He's essentially a den mother to the submissive and Dominants on staff, his softer touch perfectly complimenting Meg's harder lines. He's not her second-in-command; he's technically outside the hierarchy, which makes him able to offer a direct line of communication to both me and Meg should the situation calls for it. He doesn't intimidate people the same way we do, which paves the way for more honesty.

But that protective attitude of his keeps getting him into trouble.

"This is the second time you've inserted yourself into the

affairs of the Underworld's patrons without permission." He opens his mouth, but I raise an eyebrow. Hercules holds longer than he used to be able to, fighting himself for a solid five seconds before he wilts and lowers his eyes. I wait another beat before continuing. "You interfered with a scene between Beast, Gaeton, and Isabelle."

At that, he lifts his gaze, but only for a moment. "That was a mistake and I apologized."

"Yes, you did." Considering Isabelle wasn't a regular of the club at the time, I let that instance go without a punishment. Hercules could have used more tact when checking in on her, but he wasn't entirely wrong to do so.

The situation with Ursa, however, isn't as easy to dismiss.

"This is becoming a habit of yours. If you can't control yourself, you won't be on the club floor without Meg or myself present, and you won't have access to either employees or patrons."

His jaw drops. "You wouldn't."

I don't want to go to such extreme lengths, especially when he's slid into both our lives and the club without so much as a ripple. He *fits* here in a way I couldn't have dreamed at the start of this, and it makes him happy. I would go to significant lengths to make Hercules happy.

But I won't endanger the people who trust me to keep them safe when they come to the Underworld.

Not even for him.

Meg's hand closes on my shoulder, a light touch. Her voice, however, is as hard as it ever gets. "He would, Hercules. And if Hades makes that call, I will support him."

The betrayal on his face hurts my chest, but this can't be negotiated away. Hercules looks from Meg to me. "I don't understand. It was underhanded to give Zuri's sisters access to her, but she came here under complicated circumstances and they were worried about her."

"Hercules." I inject enough snap into my tone to straighten his spine. "Did the situation with Meg teach you nothing? Cease trying to save women who don't want to be saved. Zuri is back in Ursa's arms. She chose Ursa from the beginning. That was not your call to make." I hold up a hand when he starts to argue. "If you were that concerned about Zurielle, you should have brought it to me or Meg. We would have arranged a meeting with her sisters—with Ursa's knowledge—and ensured it all happened aboveboard. As it is, you essentially allowed a kidnapping."

His brows slam together. "That's not what happened."

Meg's hand tightens on my shoulder the slightest bit. "Zurielle was contracted with Ursa and had no desire to break that contract until *you* intervened."

"Because..." He trails off and his shoulders drop. "She came back to Ursa?"

"The first chance she got."

He stares at the ground a long moment. "I thought I was doing the right thing."

"Hercules," Meg drawls. "You didn't think at all."

He seems to steel himself and meets my gaze. "I'm to be punished."

"Yes." I don't see the point in drawing this out longer than it needs to be. "This is your second strikes, but even if I were inclined to let it go without punishment, it's not an option." I lean forward. "If this happens again, you're out."

"You'll kick me out." He goes pale.

I shake my head slowly. "No, Hercules. You're ours, and you'll remain that way, regardless of what happens with the Underworld. However, if you violate the rules again, you will be banned from the club floor, both public and private. Do you understand?"

He doesn't answer right away. Good. It means he's actually thinking things through for once. I love this impulsive, over-protective teddy bear of a man, but even I can't bend these rules for him. When he finally nods and answers, I believe the sincerity in his voice. "I understand."

"Are you ready to accept your punishment?"

"Yes, Sir."

"Good." I glance at Meg. "Please extend an invitation to Ursa for tonight. Inform her that we'd like to make an official apology."

Meg squeezes my shoulder and releases me. "Yes, Sir."

I refocus on Hercules. "I'm going to beat you, little Hercules. When I'm satisfied you've suffered enough, you're going to crawl across the public playroom and beg for Ursa's forgiveness."

"Okay," he whispers.

"Change into the black shorts, and then go kneel in the public playroom and wait for me. Position yourself in front of the St. Andrew's Cross."

"Yes, Sir." He rises on unsteady legs and exits the office.

Meg moves to perch on the edge of my desk. "Not as harsh a punishment as it could have been."

I slide my hand up her thigh. Not for seduction; simply because I like touching her. "No, not as harsh as it could have been."

"You don't bluff, Hades."

I look up and hold her gaze. "No, I don't. If he can't abide by the rules, he won't be in the Underworld."

"That will create some challenges."

I raise my brows. "Are you arguing that he should be given more leniency?"

"No." Meg huffs out a breath. "Both the Underworld and your neutral territory operate on your being able to enforce the rules. If Hercules keeps flouting them, it will undermine your authority, which makes it dangerous for everyone here."

It's exactly the conclusion I came to, but I find it strangely reassuring to hear her voice it. More and more, I've started reaching out to Meg to at least verbally walk through larger decisions. More often than not, we're in agreement, but the communication has only served to strengthen our foundations. "He has one more chance."

"I know." She leans down and brushes a light kiss against my lips. "I'll call Ursa."

I watch her walk out the door and sigh. Maybe I really am going soft in my old age, love blunting my harsh edges. I don't mind beating Hercules, or even humiliating him in front of an audience, but I'd rather do it in private.

It won't work this time, for this situation. Both punishment and apology need to be public.

It takes several hours to get everything into place. I have a monitor up of the public playroom the entire time, keeping an eye on Hercules. He obeys beautifully, kneeling with his head bowed as the room slowly fills up around him. He doesn't look up once, doesn't do more than shift a little from time to time as the stiffness sets into his body.

The study door opens and Meg slips in. "Ursa's here."

"Good." I rise and we walk together to the public playroom. It's late enough to be crowded, but early enough that people are still chatting and only engaged in minor play. Not that it matters. Those here will spread the word once things are wrapped up, and that's enough to accomplish my goals. Ursa's here, which means she intends on accepting the apology. It's enough.

I catch Meg's wrist upon entering the public playroom and pull her close enough to kiss. She submits beautifully, instantly melting and opening to me until I've had my fill. As if that will ever happen. Still, it's enough to tide me over until the end of the night. "The club is in your hands for the duration."

She smiles against my lips. "Go do your worst."

I don't respond. I simply make my way through the scattering of chairs and couches to where Hercules kneels. The conversation hushes in a wave behind me. It's been months since I've last played in public, and by now everyone knows at least some part of the story that brought us to this place. Hercules stepping out of line again. Hercules letting his shining honor get the best of him. Again.

I lace my fingers through his hair and tug his face up until I can see his eyes. "Are you ready for your punishment?"

He licks his lips. "Yes, Sir."

"Your safe word?" The question is more habit than anything else. I know it by heart.

"Olympus."

"Very well." I release him and step back. "On your feet, little Hercules."

It's a studied cruelty that keeps me in place as he struggles to his feet. I stand ready to catch him if he falls—*I* am the only one allowed to hurt Hercules—but he manages to make it to a standing position after a moment. I motion to the cross, and he obeys, moving to stand facing it and lifting his arms so I can fasten him into place. If this were any other scene, he'd be naked, but this is a punishment, so poor Hercules's cock is going to be neglected tonight.

I go to the small chest I had Meg bring out here earlier. It's got three floggers of varying weights, all picked with this punishment in mind. I weigh the first in my hand and consider him. "Remember to breathe." I don't give him a chance to respond. I simply start beating him in methodical strikes.

By the time I work over his entire back with the first flogger, he's lost some of the tension in his body. The second flogger brings it back, and I watch him closely, noting the way he clings to the cross with a white-knuckled grip.

My arm and shoulder are aching as I pick up the third flogger. This one is meant for agony, and I don't intend to use it for a prolonged period of time. I'm bringing him to the edge—not over it. Three strikes. That's all it takes for his legs to give out.

I set the flogger aside and walk to him. He twists as much as he's able and I note the tear tracts on his face. I casually wipe one with my thumb. "Are you ready to apologize?"

It takes him three tries to form words. When he finally does, his voice is haggard. "Yes, Sir."

"Good." I keep a hand at his back as I unfasten the cuffs, just in case his legs give out entirely. He wobbles a little, but doesn't collapse. I pause to squeeze the back of his neck lightly. "On your knees."

He sinks down without a word.

"Crawl to Ursa."

Whether by designer or accident, she's on the other side of the room. Hercules moves quicker than I expect considering the way his back and thighs look, but he's still obviously in pain as he reaches the couch where she reclines next to Malone. Zurielle and Alaric are nowhere in sight, but I don't blame her for leaving them at home tonight.

I stop Hercules with my hand in his hair and tug him up onto his knees. "Ursa."

"Hades."

"My submissive has something to say to you, if you're willing to hear it."

She inclines her head. "By all means."

I keep a hold of him as he draws in a ragged breath. People aren't overtly staring, but we have the attention of nearly everyone in the room. Just as I planned. Hercules shivers. "I'm sorry, Ursa. I was out of line in my conduct with your submissive. It won't happen again."

She studies him the way a predator studies a wounded animal. For a moment, I think she'll use this chance to undercut me entirely. She'd be well within her rights to do it, but the damage control will take far longer than I want to contemplate. Finally, she gives an elegant shrug. "All is forgiven, Hercules. With the understanding that if you do it again, I won't be so accommodating."

I release his hair, allowing him to bow his head. "I understand."

She glances at me. "Quite the show you put on."

"Some punishments are required to be public."

"Oh, I'm well aware." She gives me one more long look and then turns to Malone, effectively dismissing me. It's a snub, but a small one.

I pull Hercules to his feet and slide an arm around his waist. He's listing a bit, but he manages to keep his feet as we leave the public playroom and make our way back to my study. But he practically collapses onto the couch as I ease him down. I grab a blanket to wrap around him and settle down on the couch so I can pull him closer. "You did well."

He shivers and slides his arms around my waist, half in my lap. "I'm sorry, Hades. I really am. It won't happen again."

"I know, little Hercules." I sift my fingers through his

hair and tug the blanket more firmly around him. "You're forgiven."

His breath shudders out and he closes his eyes. A few moments later, his breathing evens out. I permit myself a small smile. Of course he's fallen asleep, and of course he's done it in record time. I settle back against the couch and content myself with holding him. I believe him that it won't happen again. Hercules might be misguided at times, but he has his priorities in order. He'll find other ways to help people he decides are in need. He's a knight in shining armor, after all. Not even living and loving in the Under-world is enough to tarnish *that* armor.

I wouldn't have it any other way.

THIS SHORT ORIGINALLY APPEARED AS the November 2020 short for my Patreon. Each month, patrons nominate their favorite couples and characters, vote on one, and I write a brand new short featuring the winner. For more bonus stories, please consider joining my Patreon.

16

LATE NIGHT CONVERSATIONS

AURORA

Exhaustion weighs heavily on me as the elevator ascends. It's been a long night in a string of long nights. The Underworld is busier than ever these days. Happiness looks good on the leaders of Carver City, and they're all fucking like rabbits as a result. The only one I haven't seen in a few weeks is Tink, and that's mostly because her morning sickness is turning out to be all-the-time sickness. Tomorrow's my day off, though, and I'm going to pop in with some grape popsicles and rub her feet. Hook said that's the only thing she can keep down, so I'm going to load her up.

But that's tomorrow.

The elevator eases to a stop and the doors open. I take one step out and inhale sharply. What is that I'm smelling? I inhale again, drifting farther into the penthouse I now share with Malone. I wander toward the kitchen, still sniffing and trying to identify the mouth-watering scent permeating the penthouse.

I find Malone sitting at the kitchen counter, a glass of red wine cradled in her hands, an apple pie on the stove, and stop short. "Hey. What are you doing up so late?" She's a bit of a night owl, too, but with most of her working hours in the morning, Malone is usually asleep when I get home.

She looks up, and that's when I get really worried. Her green eyes shine in the low light, and there are clear tear tracks on her face. I drop my purse and rush to her. "What's wrong? What happened? Were you *stress baking?*"

"Nothing's wrong." She gives a strange little laugh. "I'm just more affected than I thought I would be."

"You're still not making sense." I carefully extract the wine glass from her hands and set it on the counter. "What's going on?"

"The paperwork came through."

It takes my tired mind several long moments to understand what she's talking about. And when I do, *my* throat starts burning. "Already? They said it would be weeks, at least, before we heard anything."

Malone turns to me, clutching my hands. "Apparently they were wrong." Her face is too pale. I can't remember the last time she looked so freaked out, even if it's a subtle thing on Malone. "It's happening so fast. I'm not prepared."

Something in my chest pangs, but I shove it down. We've spent the last six months talking about adopting a child, had started the process and made our peace with the fact that we're in for a long wait. Even with Malone's connections and our combined wealth, these things take time.

Or at least I thought they did.

That's when I notice the file sitting at her elbow. I release one of her hands long enough to flip it open and scan the information. I frown and reread. "This says that there's two."

"An infant and a toddler. They came in together, and the agency would like to keep them together." With each word, she seems to gain more control over herself, or maybe she's just responding to my growing shock. She pulls me closer and wraps her arms around my waist. With her sitting and me standing, we're almost the same height. "We have to decide by morning."

I glance at the clock. It's five a.m. Morning is here. "You should have called the club."

"I know, but when we decided to do this, keeping your work and personal separate is one of the things we agreed on."

I know that. I'm happy with the arrangement, but this feels like a special circumstance. I let Malone hold me and stare at the pictures of the two kids. The infant is so young, still wrinkled and red. A girl. The toddler is two, a boy. He looks at the camera with large brown eyes, his hair a shock of black curls. "Two kids is a big jump. We were already talking about it eventually, but going from zero to two is huge."

"I know." She says it so carefully, as if not wanting to push me one way or another.

That tells me more than anything what she wants the answer to be. Malone is more than capable of steamrolling me when she feels like it, but she never tries it with shit like this. Important things. Life-changing things. I swallow hard. "You want them."

Her arm tightens around my waist and she exhales slowly. "Yes. But like with the initial adoption conversation, this isn't something where there's a compromise available. We either say yes or we say no. We cannot have one without the other."

"I would never ask that." My gaze drifts back to the pictures. How many times did I wish for a sibling when I was growing up? Someone who *got it* in a way the adults around me never did. Someone who would have my back and I'd have theirs. It was a childish fantasy at the time—I know better than to think sibling relationships are without complications—but apparently the remnants haven't quite left me. "They shouldn't be separated."

I relax against her and close my eyes. This is a big decision, but is it really? We knew from the start that we wanted kids—as in multiple—and maybe this isn't quite the route we'd decided on, but the end result is still the same. I wrap my arms around Malone and slide my fingers through her short hair. "Hey."

She pulls me a little closer and her lips curve. "Hi."

"I love you. You know that, right?"

Malone dips her hands beneath my tank top and lightly grips my hips. "I love you, too."

That's what it comes down to. We love each other. The last year hasn't been without its hiccups, but our feelings have never changed and, if anything, they've only gotten stronger. We've found compromise after compromise that works for both of us, and we've created a life that *works*. One where we're happy. Really fucking happy. I smile. "Let's do it. If you're onboard, then I'm onboard."

She goes so still, I'm not sure she's breathing. "Are you sure?"

I answer as honestly as I can. "I'm a little freaked out, but I think it's just nerves. I'd be freaked out no matter when this happened because it's such a *big* step. No matter how sure I am, of course I'm going to be nervous about a big life change like adopting a kid. But that doesn't mean I don't want to do it. I do." I give a shaky laugh. "What first-time parent isn't nervous, even if they did the whole pregnancy thing? Tink and Hook are a fucking mess, and they are going to be amazing parents."

"I'm nervous, too." She says it so softly, it's barely above a whisper. "My mother was a good mother, but she wasn't exactly warm. What if I damage them?"

Strangely enough, her nerves calm mine. I cup her face with my hands. She might not be warm, but that's not all there is to life. "Malone, you are one of the most caring people I know. You're going to be a great mother."

"Are you sure?"

We've had this conversation before. Multiple times. We both have plenty of baggage to bring to the table, though Malone's upbringing wasn't exactly deprived of love. But Sabine Valley is a different breed, and she's achingly aware of that since we started talking about kids. I press a light kiss to her lips. "If you aren't sure, we can wait."

Her grip tightens on me. "I don't want to wait." Already, there's a possessive thread in her tone, and it makes me smile as she says, "I'm sure."

I let loose a light laugh. "Then let's do this." It's not as simple as that, but even before we put in the paperwork to prepare for the adoption process, we had a plan for what parenthood would look like with the two of us. I'll cut back my hours in the Underworld and Malone will delegate a little more aggressively to create time on her end as well. We haven't outfitted the spare bedroom into a child's bedroom, but we have a full list of all the things we'll need, as well as decorating choices because... of course we do.

Malone kisses me, and I can feel her confidence settling through her again, piece by piece. It might be strange that her doubt makes me love her more, but I'm so glad we talked through this. I feel fucking *good* about this. I lift my head enough to say, "When do we let them know?"

"In about an hour." She presses one last kiss to my lips and guides me back a step. "Have you eaten anything since I saw you last?"

My skin heats and I can't quite hold her gaze. "It was a busy night." And I don't normally like to eat meals while I'm on shift. It's easier to inhale a power bar or something like that.

"Thought so." She gives my ass a squeeze and releases me. "Go take a shower and I'll heat up some egg drop soup for you."

My stomach chooses that moment to growl and I laugh a little. "Sounds good." I take one step away and hesitate. "Malone?"

"Yes?"

"I'm really, really happy." Happier than I ever could have dreamed. It still blows my mind a little bit that I've found this with *Malone*, but I wouldn't change a thing for the world.

Her smile is warm and wide. "I'm happy, too. Now, go take that shower." She lets out a surprisingly light laugh. "We're about to be parents."

ABOUT THE AUTHOR

Katee Robert is a *New York Times* and USA Today bestselling author of contemporary romance and romantic suspense. *Entertainment Weekly* calls her writing "unspeakably hot." Her books have sold over a million copies. She lives in the Pacific Northwest with her husband, children, a cat who thinks he's a dog, and two Great Danes who think they're lap dogs.

www.kateerobert.com